F   Gollin, James.
GOL
           Broken consort

$15.95

DATE			

© THE BAKER & TAYLOR CO.

BROKEN
CONSORT

Other Antiqua Players mysteries by James Gollin:

The Verona Passamezzo
Eliza's Galiardo
The Philomel Foundation

JAMES GOLLIN

BROKEN CONSORT

ST. MARTIN'S PRESS
NEW YORK

Design by Maura Fadden Rosenthal

Library of Congress Cataloging-in-Publication Data

Gollin, James.
    Broken consort / James Gollin.
      p. cm.
    ISBN 0-312-03298-6
    I. Title.
    PS3557.O445B76   1989
    813'.54—dc20   89-30427
                                         CIP

First Edition

10 9 8 7 6 5 4 3 2 1

*For Mary and Tim, Cheryl and Doug
with love*

BROKEN
CONSORT

C H A P T E R I

*I*ncarnación was messing around in front of the building when I went out with the mail, which was the third bill from us to a small college in New Jersey for services rendered. Even for money-starved small colleges, this one was unusually shameless. They owed us fifteen hundred dollars, and I thanked God I'd insisted on the first fifteen hundred up front.

I dropped the bill in the mailbox on the corner and walked back the half block to the building, my head hunched into the collar of my raincoat, my feet in their rubbers schlooping wetly on the decaying sidewalk. Where else in the world does winter rain assault you like enemy shrapnel, I wondered, except on Amsterdam Avenue in New York City?

Incarnación was still out there when I got back. He'd tied the dog of Ramón the super to one of the two brass stanchions that held up the building's awning, tattered but proud testimony to our respectability. He was listlessly rubbing a blackened polishing rag up and down the other stanchion.

The dog flattened its ears and bared its teeth soundlessly at me, straining at its leash.

"What's wrong?" I asked. "Hasn't he had his delivery boy today?"

"Ey! Come on Mr. French, you know he don't bite." Incarnación looked at me and his face brightened. He carefully rolled up his indescribable rag and balanced it on top of his can of Noxon. Then he wiped his hands on his green work pants. I waited to see what he had in mind. Incarnación is Ramón the super's nephew and business associate. The business is automotive reassembly. At least, that's Incarnación's name for the twenty-four-hour-a-day operation in smoking-hot auto parts, imports only, that the two of them run out of about six of the tenant storage bins in the basement.

I knew there had to be something, because otherwise Incarnación wouldn't be wasting precious time on a mere tenant like me.

His smile faded and he shook his head solemnly. "You know," he said, "it's really too bad about that Mrs. Rosensweig in twelve-A. She was a really nice old lady."

"What happened to her?"

"You didn't know? Cancer. She was sick for a long time and then just the other day . . . She was really nice. And listen, you know, she had nobody, she was all alone. The city had to come and take her away. And you know, she got some really nice things up in her apartment, nobody wants them."

"Oh?"

"Yeah—hey," he interrupted himself as if inspiration had just visited him, which I strongly suspected was not the case. "You're a musician. She got a real nice piano up there, Mrs. Rosensweig. Big huge thing, dark brown, real nice wood, looks like it could be walnut, you know. We gotta take it down tonight, make room up there, probably gonna sell it. Maybe you wanna look at it?"

The look on his face was so innocently persuasive, I

almost said yes, but then I began to think about what it would mean. Namely, unlawfully entering dead Mrs. Rosensweig's gloomy premises, upon which the soot had no doubt already begun to settle, from which all the smaller valuables would already have been liberated to the basement, and in which, no matter what Incarnación and his uncle Ramón said, we had no business being, to make an offer on one of the bigger items these guys were getting ready to steal.

Besides, in my musical life a grand piano was about the last thing I needed. "No, thanks, Incarnación," I said. I quickly added, "But thank you for thinking of me." You don't want to be rude to your super's nephew. Not in our building, you don't.

"Hey, no problem," he said cheerfully. "If you change your mind the next few days, just let me know."

Promising him I would, I escaped into the elevator.

Jackie was practicing when I let myself into the apartment, and the phone was ringing steadily. I hurried into the kitchen to answer it, wondering as always how she managed to ignore all distractions, even ringing telephones, and just stay locked inside her music.

"Antiqua Players," I said into the receiver.

"Er . . . is this Alan French?"

I admitted to being Alan French.

"Mr. French, my name is Steve Hundley. From Flourishing Arts. I wonder if you remember me."

Something stirred sluggishly in my midbrain, but I wasn't sure what, so I grunted noncommittally.

"We're an arts coordinating group," Steve Hundley said. "Your group is registered with us."

"We are?"

"Oh yes, several years ago. You must remember."

It was possible. The city is full of struggling little arts organizations that try to find bookings for struggling little actors, dancers, magicians, jugglers, clowns, mimes, and musicians. In my younger and hungrier days, I might well have signed us up with this one.

3

"Well, anyway," Hundley went on, "I'm assuming you still are. Registered, I mean. Because we've got a gig for you."

I really hate that term. "You mean, an engagement?"

"Yes. It's a private social. The date is Saturday, March eighth. They want about an hour and a quarter program, instrumental only, and they specifically asked for you."

"Hang on," I said, "I'll get our calendar." I went into the studio. Jackie was still practicing, but she looked up and smiled at me. There was nothing in our datebook for Saturday the eighth of March. "A private social," I said to Hundley. "Does that mean we have to mix with the guests afterward?"

"That's up to you, but you'll probably want to. I mean, there's drinks and supper and most of our artists do like to make an appearance."

"Well, we're past the drinks-and-supper stage," I said.

"I'm sure you are," Hundley said tactfully. "But are you interested, and if you are, can you tell me about how much your group would charge?"

"Our fee for a private evening program is fifteen hundred dollars," I said, the slow-pay Jerseyites in my mind.

The price I was quoting was far from cheap, and I figured it would end the conversation right there, but Hundley surprised me. "We get twenty percent," he said, "so you'd net out twelve hundred. Would you do it for that?"

"No," I said.

"Okay, then I'll tell them seventeen hundred; you pay us three forty and you wind up with thirteen sixty. How's that?"

"No," I said.

"How about if I tell them eighteen fifty, you pay us three seventy, and you net out fourteen eighty."

"Fifteen hundred," I said.

"Oh shit," Hundley said, a little tiredly, "you win. They pay eighteen fifty and you give us three fifty."

"Roger," I said. "They sign a contract and pay us in full, in advance." No more New Jersey fiascos this season. "Then you get paid."

"How do I know—"

4

"Simple," I said. "They make out the check to me, messenger it to you, and we go to my bank together."

"Roger-dodger," Hundley said.

"Before you go, you better tell me who this is that we're playing for."

"Yes, of course. It's Jeremiah T. B. G. Boyle."

CHAPTER 2

ell, Lordy be, Jeremiah Boyle," said Ralph Mitchell brightly a few hours later. "It will be celebrityville for a night, that's for sure. I wouldn't miss it for the world. Do I play one of his harpsichords or do I bring my own?"

"We'll find out," I said. "It's for March eighth. Jackie and I are free. Ralph's free. How about you, David?"

"I'm in," David said, helping himself to at least six of Jackie's chocolate chip cookies.

"Terry?"

Terry looked worried. "That's a Saturday, right?"

I nodded.

"Let me make a phone call." Terry got up from the sofa and disappeared into the kitchen. A minute later, he returned. "It's okay," he said. "My cousin Guy's home from Williams that weekend, he'll cover for me."

"Guy?" I asked.

Terry shrugged. "It's Guido, naturally, but what can I tell you? Williams is giving him fancy ideas."

"I wish your uncle would close up Monza's and retire," Jackie said darkly. "It would solve a lot of your problems."

By now, I'm sure you don't need telling that we the aforementioned are musicians. But I should probably be more specific and inform you that, jointly and severally, we are the Antiqua Players. There are five of us, all instrumentalists, and for nearly nine years we've been performing early music together on the instruments for which it was created.

Ralph Mitchell has already tipped you off that he's our harpsichordist. David the Cookie Monster is David Brodkey; his specialty is the lute. Terry Monza plays woodwinds, and so do I. But my remorselessly practical mother made me study violin as well as flute, and I also play the viols and other early bowed strings. In fact, because we needed to give ourselves flexibility as an ensemble, we've all learned how to get along on more than one instrument.

Even Jackie.

As far as the rest of us are concerned, Jackie Craine needn't bother with anything but her viola da gamba.

The viola da gamba is the older cousin of the cello. It sits between the player's knees. Its fingerboard is fretted, not smooth like the fingerboard of a cello, and it has six strings instead of four. The gamba bow curves away from the hair and you hold it from beneath, which evens out the stroke. Play the gamba badly and it whines at you like a bratty teenager. Play it the way Jackie plays it, and look the way she looks when she does it, and your only competitor, an elderly gentleman in Zurich named Heinrich Wunschler, will retire from the concert stage.

Yours truly leads the Antiqua Players, but Jackie, in a word, is our star, and a main reason we're one of the more flourishing early music ensembles. She's tall and slender, and her long dark hair, beautiful arms and hands, and expressive face don't hurt on the platform. But she could be old and ugly and it wouldn't matter. She's so secure technically that the rest of us almost take her for granted. She's so interesting musically that I sometimes forget my own part in a piece because I'm listening to her. And personally, Jackie Craine is a wonder among musicians. She never lies. She never pouts or throws rehearsal tantrums or threatens to quit. If she says she'll do a thing, she does it. Her checkbook balances, her insurance is up to date, her coffee is delicious, and when the neighbors hear her practicing late at night they pound on the ceiling and beg her not to stop.

Okay, I'm partial. Part of the reason, I must admit, is that in her spare time, of which there's never enough, Jackie Craine manages to be a wonderfully tender Mrs. Alan French.

When we started, the revival of medieval and Renaissance music had barely begun. We were lucky to play together a few times a year. A job at a slow-paying small college in the wilds of New Jersey would have been a major event in our musical lives, and any fee larger than seventy-five dollars would have been a godsend. Now, of course, early music is a Movement. Hundreds if not thousands of fanatics scrape away daily on rebecs, clout odd-shaped drums, and make quaint sounds, destroying their lip and lung tissue in the process, on shawms, recorders, rauschpfeiffen, krummhorns, cornets, and sackbuts. There are even Schools of Thought. Not long ago at a symposium I was actually grabbed and punched, rather weakly I must admit, by a baroque oboist infuriated by a remark I'd made—disparaging, he thought—about "authenticity."

Mostly we steer clear of all the infighting. We don't dress up in costume to play, or insist on meantone tuning, or perform only on instruments built within weeks of the day the music was supposedly written. We hold to the peculiar idea that beautiful music of whatever period will sound beautiful today if it gets careful study, imaginative instrumentation, plenty of rehearsing, and polished performance.

This earns the Antiqua Players a goodly share of the early music action in New York and environs. Twice a year we actually fill Alice Tully Hall. Our reviews are encouraging.

But even though we've been making a little money, we all have to do other things in music in order to survive.

I play in theater orchestras and pickup recording sessions.

Ralph does a two-day-a-week stint as accompanist in a ballet school known to us all as The Barn. He and I both teach. Jackie teaches too. She used to have to drag herself out to Long Island, but now she's turning pupils away from her viol master classes here in town.

David refuses to teach. "What do I need with the aggravation?" he asks lucidly. The girls who cluster around him keep him fed, clothed, and sheltered most of the time. In amatory emergencies, he seeks out Jake, a decrepit luthier on the Lower East Side. Jake will lend him money and lie fluently to his women about his whereabouts. In return, David has to put in time repairing the fragile guitars Jake's customers are always buying at ridiculous prices, mishandling, and destroying.

Terry? When he's not with us, he's at Monza's, in Queens. Terry claims it's the only gourmet Italian restaurant in the borough, and if the size of the portions and the size of the jammed parking lot are any indications, he's absolutely right. But the best thing about Monza's from Terry's point of view is not the quality of the cuisine; it's that his uncle owns it and has lately been beseeching Terry to take it over. From our point of view, this is not so great, because it makes Terry restless. We want what's right for Terry, of course. Jackie, Ralph, David, and I agree that he *should* leave the Antiqua Players for the restaurant business.

Maybe. Sometime. Eventually.

But not right now.

Anyway, there you have us. And now that you know what we do, you can see why we're in no position to turn up our noses at fifteen hundred dollars for a private musicale, a party at which one of the attractions for the guests is the opportunity to mingle with—and fuss over—real live musical talent.

"This Jeremiah," David said. "I know he's famous. Is he loaded, or what?"

"Don't talk with your mouth full," said Jackie. "And yes, Jeremiah is loaded."

"Not exactly," I said knowingly. It's not that I'm on intimate terms with New York's high and mighty, but my dentist subscribes to *New York* magazine, and the last time I was in (X rays and two cavities, ninety dollars) I read its profile of Jeremiah Boyle.

Jeremiah Ten Brinck Gardner Boyle isn't poor, God knows. But it's not his share of his clan's mining money that makes him famous, it's his own brains, personality, and devouring ambition to *be* famous. Over the years, he's used the money very skillfully. It's helped him make the slippery climb from skinny-kid–maverick journalist all the way up to syndicated columnist, arbiter of taste, TV celebrity, and adviser to the great. It's helped him to do, and to be seen doing, all sorts of fun things along the way, from collecting Chinese art to playing high-goal polo in Palm Beach, from starting a scholarship program for gifted black children to running unsuccessfully for the U.S. Senate in New York. And now that Jeremiah Boyle is at the very top of the charts, so to speak, the money helps keep him there.

"Never mind rich," Ralph said. "What are we going to play?"

"You're certainly going to have to give them something special," Jackie said.

"I know it," said Ralph.

"You think all that stuff is really true?" Terry grabbed the last of the cookies. "About him playing the harpsichord?"

"I've heard yes and I've heard no," Ralph said.

One of the more interesting pieces of the Boyle legend is the tale that Jeremiah Boyle, when he's not busy running the universe, is a serious amateur of the harpsichord. How serious? He's supposed to have studied with Landowska as a kid, and with various other virtuosi since, and there are always rumors drifting around about which gifted young harpsichord builders and players he's backing this year. True or not, the stories make entertaining gossip.

"I don't believe it," Terry said lazily, "I think it's just part of his Renaissance Man act, like the polo and the fencing."

"What do you want to play at this thing, Ralph?" I said, to avoid argument. Also, my mind was beginning to focus on the programming pitfalls of a performance for a small private audience.

"Haven't a clue. Nothing too long and hard, though. Why? Do you have something in mind?"

"I do, as a matter of fact," I said.

"Tell."

"I'd like to do a seventeenth-century evening," I said. "Half an hour of English, half an hour of French. We could open with the 'Miserere.'" Despite its title, this was a surprisingly lively Jacobean piece for harpsichord with gamba accompaniment. "Then we could do a Coperario—"

"How about a Holborne suite?" Terry asked.

"Maybe. Lots of brass groups play Holborne. I was thinking of some Hume for lute and viol . . ."

As usual, everybody got into the act. About the time the coffee gave out, my idea of having Ralph and Jackie start off was scrapped in favor of opening with something from Thomas Morley's *Consort Lessons*, in which we'd all play.

"I'll cut it down from six instruments to five," I said, "and score it"—I scribbled on the back of the phone bill—"for lute, gamba, two tenor recorders, and baroque flute. *Then* the 'Miserere' and then . . ."

Long before we were through, we had to send out to Uncle Weng's.

This neighborhood is gentrifying with deadly haste. Last week a boutique that offers cotton and silk jeans for four hundred dollars a pair replaced our dry cleaner. There's still a supermarket, but it's flanked by one of those very austere pasta, cheese, and extra-extra-virgin olive oil emporiums where there's a cover charge to stand in the checkout line.

Uncle Weng's, however, will not suffer itself to be uprooted from its home on Broadway. One reason is that it's housed in a storefront so narrow it's almost invisible. A second is that Weng owns the storefront. A third is that Weng's looks so crummy the affluent denizens of the New West Side hurry past it. Weng likes it that way. One of the waiters swore to us that Weng keeps a jar of special roaches, "big like crayfish," to drop in the soup of any food editor who ventures inside.

"How can you tell if a customer is a food editor?" Terry was rash enough to demand.

"Fat person wearing wash-and-wear blouse with party of four, never been in before, food editor. If not, give roaches anyway."

Uncle Weng's special corn soup quickly produced consensus on the first half of the program, but the battle over the second half, the French half, lasted all the way through the spicy bean curd with broccoli and well into the Szechuan garlic pork.

"Okay," I said at about ten thirty, while David was crunching down the last of the fortune cookies. "Does anybody want to run through any of this stuff?"

"You have been working too hard and are in need of a rest," David intoned.

"Let me see that." I made a grab for the fortune, but he wadded it up and stuck it in a pocket.

"Really, though, won't tomorrow do?" Ralph said. "I really should get back and be with Cat Frescobaldi." Cat Frescobaldi was Ralph's newest and trendiest acquisition, a ring-tailed, tortoiseshell Maine coon. She was more cross-eyed, shyer and if possible dumber than a Persian, but I must admit she was gorgeous. Ralph liked to think she got upset if he was away for too long.

"Fine, go ahead," I sighed. "How about you, David? . . . David?"

David was standing by the window, peering out at Amsterdam Avenue.

"What's wrong?" asked Jackie.

"Do you see anybody . . . waiting out there?"

Jackie joined him. "No, I don't see anybody."

"You see what I mean, the person in, like, the black raincoat? In the doorway?"

"There's nobody *in* the doorway, David."

"No, over there. I think it's Simone."

Jackie laughed. "David, don't be silly. It's raining cats and dogs. Simone's home in bed in Valley Stream."

David shook his head. "She's been calling me a lot. Listen, I don't mind staying for a while. Maybe we should rehearse something."

Jackie and I looked at each other.

"I wouldn't mind," David said, "but she cries all the time. It gets on my nerves." David has no nerves.

"Stick around," I said. "We'll play a little and then you can have the back bedroom."

In the end Ralph and Terry stayed, too, and we put in two solid hours of rehearsal for a Valentine's Day concert at a church in Chappaqua.

CHAPTER 3

ood evening," I said in my most dulcet tones to Jeremiah T. B. G. Boyle and his fifty or so assembled guests. "I can't imagine a more delightful place in which to play the program we've planned for tonight." I couldn't, either. After introducing us, I went right into my spiel about music in seventeenth-century England and music in seventeenth-century France and how they differed and yet were the same.

In the background, I could hear the rain beating, but beating in a very mannerly way so as not to offend, on the windows and roof of the house. Boyle's house, so said the tasteful bronze plaque on an exterior wall, was a landmark: one of a row of eight brick houses on Henderson Place, an odd little enclave of yesteryear far east on Eighty-sixth near the river. Fortunes have been spent in Henderson Place to make the houses look like cozy Old New York on the outside and New New York within. I wouldn't know about the other houses, but to judge from his combination living room and library, Boyle, or someone in the family, had more than gotten his money's worth.

We were there to play the music, not to chat about it, so I kept my lecture short. When I was finished speaking the audience rustled politely and settled its collective bottoms on the rented chairs. I took my own seat, set my one-keyed wooden flute to my lip, glanced around to catch everybody's eye, and gave the upbeat.

Don't ask me why, but from the first note on I had a feeling that this was going to be an interesting evening.

The Morley went well enough. Instead of his usual lute, David was playing his chitarrone, a huge impressive-looking archlute he'd acquired in Italy. The booming sounds he got out of its brass bottom strings blended wonderfully with Jackie's gamba. Ralph and Terry were both supposed to be playing tenor recorder, but at the last minute we'd substituted a great bass recorder for Ralph's tenor. It too looked and sounded impressive. The effect we were trying for was a kind of jovial dialogue between Terry's recorder and my flute, with a nice full bass to underpin the exchange.

The only tricky part of the whole piece is a rather Italianate passage near the end where Terry and I charge up and down the scale a couple of times in thirds. We'd mangled it three times in a row in rehearsal that afternoon, but this time we negotiated it smoothly and the others came in under us for the final bars.

Okay, Jeremiah Boyle's friends aren't the kind who whistle and stamp their feet. But they do clap. They did clap. But it would have been nice, I thought, if they'd been just a bit more demonstrative.

Maybe Ralph and Jackie could heat them up.

Tonight had been one of Ralph's better nights. By this I mean that he hadn't spent the hour before the performance huddled in a bathroom, pallid and retching. His hands had been icy cold and shaking as usual, so he'd kept his sheepskin mittens on until the last minute. But he hadn't gone completely green, and he'd even managed a feeble grin at some feeble joke one of us had tossed at him.

Now he seated himself at the harpsichord as tranquilly as if he'd never known stage fright in his life.

Jackie switched chairs with Terry to be closer to Ralph. She had on a dark gray wool jersey dress with a long skirt. Short skirts and the gamba simply don't go together, but there's no reason a dress with a long skirt can't have a top that fits like a second skin, which I'm pleased to say this one did.

The audience waited.

Ralph dislikes obvious signals. His eyebrows went up, then down, and they began the "Miserere."

In the first four bars alone, there are fourteen twiddly little ornaments for the harpsichordist's right hand, with dozens more to follow. Some of them lie in ambush on weak beats; others are sprinkled in two's and three's, leaving no time to relax the hand in preparation. These tiny slides and trills are what give this piece—and as far as that goes, most harpsichord music—its character. Leave them out and the tune goes naked. Play them badly and they're as obtrusive as hiccups.

Ralph not only played them mechanically correctly, he fitted them together so they stopped being merely decorative and instead became a second part to the music. I'd heard him do it a dozen times before, but this time it struck me that for all its cheeriness the "Miserere" was a religious work after all. Its composer, whoever he was, meant the main tune to stand for God's handiwork; the ornaments, for man's.

A toe bit painfully into my right ankle.

A recital platform, believe me, is no place to sit dreamily contemplating the profundity of one's insights into music.

The toe was Terry's delicate way of reminding me that Jackie and Ralph were well into their last repeat. There would be applause, but the way we'd rehearsed it, Jackie and Ralph were going to stay seated and as the applause started to fade I'd join in and we'd play right through into the next piece, a suite for three instruments. It's a simple little trick we sometimes use to build up momentum. It would work to-night, too, if only Alan French would awaken from his trance, grab his next instrument and be ready. It would also help if the audience would go on clapping, which to my irritation it wasn't doing.

Nonchalant but sweating slightly, I grabbed. Ralph, overriding the audience according to plan, was already in the third bar of his four-bar lead. Jackie was poised, ready to make her entry. I had two seconds to settle the treble viol on my lap, get into the swing and three and four and go!

Ralph, poker-faced, gave four tiny bobs of his head, his insulting way of making sure I had the beat.

I studiously avoided Jackie's eye.

Why did Terry's cousin Guido at Williams want to be called Guy? Because he thought it made him sound classier. Nearly four hundred years ago, for exactly the same reason, the Elizabethan composer John Cooper, back in London from a tour of Italy, had reversed the process. He'd renamed himself Giovanni Coperario. *His* name-change evidently helped: Cooper-Coperario landed the job of music teacher to the two young sons of James I.

Musicologists call Coperario a transitional composer. For *transitional*, read "mixed up in a weird way we don't understand." The suite we were performing, for viols and keyboard, opens with a fantasia, very English stuff, and moves on to an alman, which is a French treatment of a German dance form, and winds up with an ayre, which is an English version of a French treatment of an Italian song form. Luckily for us and our audiences, the music is lovely.

At about bar twenty of the fantasia, I gave up and looked straight at Jackie.

Her lips twitched, and on her next entry she slowed down a hair and leaned on the first note as if to say, "There, you poor thing, you can't miss *that*."

Hmmph. My entry overlapped and echoed hers, and I made sure to play just harshly enough to blur the end of her phrase.

Ralph didn't do anything, but he looked over at me sharply, perfectly well aware of what I was up to.

If we'd been seriously annoyed with one another, we'd have turned our performance into a cutting session, and since I'm meaner than either Ralph or Jackie I probably would have won. But of course nobody was mad at anybody. All I was really saying was, Now, now, don't mess around too much with Papa Bear.

We calmed down, finished the fantasia in amicable partnership, and polished off the alman and ayre with proper spirit.

Once again, the applause pattered forth politely. I didn't have to exchange glances with the others. I knew we were all thinking the same depressing thought: What a bunch of fish on ice.

David came forward, looking shy, to play his lute solo.

David is, of course, not shy. Nor is he frail and delicate like the lute itself. But somehow he manages to create the impression that he's all of these things. Maybe it's the tender way he takes the lute in his arms and the soulful gaze he directs at it before he begins to play. Or maybe it's the lock of dark hair that tumbles artlessly over his forehead as he bends to his beloved instrument. Whatever it is, audiences eat him up. And of course David is a damn good lutenist. He has the fingers and he has the touch, which on the lute really does have to be light. Usually it isn't. Our unfriendly competitor James Weede is a case in point. James is head of the James Weede Consorte and Rumba Bande (we call it that because of James's predilection for adding strange percussion instruments like maracas to his medieval renderings). Anyway, James *strums* the lute, but David, by merely caressing its double string courses with his fingers, gets more sound out of it and makes it sing.

The people gave David what I've heard described as a nice little hand. And this brought us to the last number before intermission, a pair of masque ayres by Matthew Locke.

In the first one we all played recorders. Then, just for

fun, we switched to strings, having rented two tenor viols
from Jake the luthier for the occasion. Jackie played the
gamba, which is the bass viol, David and Ralph did their best
on the tenors, Terry tackled the alto, and I played the little
pardessus. We'd worked hard on this piece in rehearsal, but I
have to be honest and admit that it didn't come out too well
that night in performance. There were no real clunkers, but
Ralph of all people lost his place and had to drop out for two
measures and the ending was sloppy. Very sloppy.

The audience saw us offstage very quietly indeed.

"Oh God," Ralph moaned, "what's *wrong* with these
people?" We'd repaired to the little sitting room adjoining the
library that we'd been given as a green room.

"Shhh," Jackie said.

"Yeah," Terry said, "you might wake somebody."

"You're right," said Ralph. "I might even wake our
Fearless Leader."

"Okay, okay," I said, "I was dreaming there, I admit it."

"You do?" Jackie said.

"No," I said.

Everyone laughed.

"Anyway, why pick on me?" I said. "Ralph—"

"You *conned* me into playing that thing," Ralph said
defensively. "You said I had a natural gift for strings. It was a
totally dumb idea."

"I don't think so," I said, mildly for me. "But you're
probably right, we're never going to turn you into the Heifetz
of the tenor viol."

"Wait a minute," Ralph said, suddenly switching sides.
"Are you insinuating—"

"He's not insinuating anything," Jackie said. "He's telling you. The viol is not your thing. And you won't have to play
it anymore, either, because the Locke is O-U-T *out* from now
on."

"Hold it," I said, not mildly at all. "That's not up to you
to decide."

"Hey," David said.

We stopped arguing.

"Yes, David?" Ralph said carefully.

"The potato chips are great. Have some."

The big bowl of chips passed from hand to hand. Coke cans were snapped open. All who were not playing woodwinds in the rest of the program, which is to say Jackie, Ralph, and David, indulged themselves.

"Look at this," said Terry.

"Disgusting," I agreed. "Straight out of Gomorrah. Gratifying their appetites while we look on and suffer."

"Seriously," Ralph said, "can I not play the tenor viol anymore?"

"I had hopes," I said.

"I know, the Guarnieri Viol Consort, but—"

"You're probably right," I said, "it's not going to work. Oh, well, another dream shattered."

"Not to mention my nerves," Ralph said with a smile. It was his charming way of apologizing for playing badly.

"Look," Jackie said, "let's go out and do a good second half and talk about this later."

"Good," I said. I peered out the door. "They're back. Maybe they never got up. Everybody ready? Jackie first, Ralph next, Terry, David, and me."

We opened the French half of the program with a plaintive tourdion and two quick branles, peasant dances prettied up for use by the nobility during the great dance craze that swept over northern Europe early in the sixteenth century. Nice appealing music. We played it well, thank God, well enough to blur if not blot out the memory of the screwed-up piece for viols.

Then came Jackie, and she redeemed our reputation forever.

Her big piece for the evening was a suite of dances for gamba and accompanying harpsichord by Marin Marais, who was to the viola da gamba roughly what Bunny Berigan was to the swing cornet: a supreme exponent of elegance. What makes the Marais a big piece is its sheer demands on technique.

The knottiest problems come right in its opening movement, a prelude, or, as Ralph calls it, "music to drop your program by." Marais wrote a classic French-style overture, well larded with double-dotted sixteenths and thick chords. These sound nice and dramatic in full orchestra, but they're wicked to articulate on the gamba, or any other bowed instrument. Jackie had been fooling with the prelude for months, trying to find an approach that didn't make it sound like a slightly top-heavy circus float.

Her answer that night was beautifully simple. Instead of setting her teeth and whacking the chords hard and loud each time, she eased off and took them softly. The change was remarkable. Rather than lurching along, the music seemed to relax. In the place of florid declamation, Jackie put shadow and mystery.

By the time she was halfway through, I was kicking myself that we hadn't brought along a tape recorder.

She chased away shadow and mystery in the quick, cheerful allemande and courante that followed and brought them back in the much slower sarabande. Then, like a storyteller who interrupts one good tale to tell an even better one, Jackie turned to the rondeau.

Rondeaux, cribbed from folk music, are deliberately quaint and pastoral. This particular one has five slight little tunes, the couplets, plus a refrain to be repeated after every couplet. In Jackie's hands, the thing turned into an exquisite conversation. Her turns of phrase, subtle pauses, and ornaments made the couplets variously gossipy, polite, ribald, sad, and romantic. The refrain somehow became the voice of an earnest, polite, but faintly bewildered interlocutor, asking over and over again, Did they really? Are you sure?

She let the final plaintive repeat of the refrain die away. And suddenly she whirled back into the suite proper, into the gigue, playing each strain fast the first time through and lightning fast on the repeat and finishing with a lusty upward slide, a flurry of triplets, and a perfect quadruple-stop close.

The audience unfroze like snow on a sunny morning. Elderly ladies smiled delightedly and nodded as they clapped. One bejeweled dowager actually thumped her walking stick on the floor several times in token of her approval. The younger women and men too were clapping. Boyle himself stood to lead the applause. "Brava! Bravi!" he exclaimed, "Brava! Bravi!" My God, I thought. *Brava* is for Jackie the female, *bravi* is for Jackie and Ralph together, and *brava-bravi* is to let *us* know that Jeremiah Boyle knows the right way to cheer.

"Go on," I said to Jackie, making little *get up* gestures. "Take your bow, you've saved our ass, you were marvelous."

She rose, flushed and smiling, made Ralph stand, then moved to his side and gave him a quick hug: all unrehearsed, spontaneous and from the heart. And she was right, because as brilliant as Jackie had been, Ralph had been equally brilliant, responding instantly to her mood in the prelude, staying with her in the dances and the rondeau and matching her virtuosity in the gigue.

Everybody in the audience clapped some more, and I clapped too.

Needless to say, we sailed through the remainder of the program, drawing warm applause for every number. We wound up with one encore, a long one, an air from a suite by François Couperin. I'd gone through a lot of music paper arranging it so that everyone could take a twelve-bar solo, but it was well worth the effort.

Back in our improvised green room, Jackie set down her gamba, let out a deep breath, pushed her hair back from her forehead, and gave us an enormous smile of pure relief.

"Wow," said Terry.

"I entirely agree," I said.

"Yeah, you were really good," David said. "Who ate all the potato chips?"

"I wouldn't worry, David," Ralph said tiredly, stuffing music into his briefcase. "There's bound to be more outside."

CHAPTER 4

The first person to approach us when we went out to mingle was the great man himself.

The famous Jeremiah Boyle jawline was starting to go slack now, and the flesh under the eyes was puffier than I'd expected, but I must admit that Boyle had every right to be pleased with what he saw in the mirror. In real life, that narrow Irish face of his, with its beaky nose and pointed chin, turned out to have the same sleek ferrety handsomeness that came across so tellingly on the tube. The hair was trimmed longer than in Boyle's enfant terrible days, and it was graying, but there was plenty of it. It made him look distinguished, and if anything more youthful.

Boyle didn't bother to introduce himself; he clearly felt he didn't have to. He just let fly, in a drawing room version of the North Shore honk he'd made famous across the country and around the world. "Well, God! You must be hungry and thirsty after all of that, not to mention exhausted! Cyril . . . over here!"

The brimming glasses on Cyril's silver tray were crystal. They were also at least twice as big as normal champagne glasses. We each took one.

"Well, cheers," Boyle said. "The Widow's wonderful, isn't she, after a hard night's work."

The Widow? What was Boyle talking about? A dim memory of an ad I'd seen somewhere gave me a hint. La Veuve Clicquot, the Widow Clicquot, was supposed to have invented champagne. "Um," I mumbled. "She certainly is."

"Now," Boyle said, "you must tell me all about what happened. And by the way, congratulations." He turned to Jackie. "That was a *wonderful* performance. Absolutely bravura. And you too. It's *Ralph* Mitchell, am I right?"

Jackie smiled politely and Ralph nodded. I could tell he was storing up Boyle's mannerisms and speech habits for future reference.

"Now," Boyle repeated, "I'm dying to find out why that ending was so ragged—but I'm being rude to my other guests, aren't I? Hello, Libbie!" he called across the room. "You have to let me introduce you to people," he told us. "Later. Please have another drink. Have more than one. I'll be back!"

We watched him go.

"Boy," Terry said, "he works the crowd like a pro."

He did, too, moving from knot of people to knot of people, patting a shoulder, putting his arm briefly around a woman, even exchanging laughs and high fives with one guest, a tall black man who might have been anything from a sportscaster to an investment banker.

Boyle didn't come right back, of course, but it hardly mattered. Other people kept drifting up to thank us and staying on to talk. In the case of some of the males, the idea clearly was to have a better look at Jackie. The females were less lucky. After a few minutes David had wandered off in search of edible refreshment and had promptly been waylaid by a very tall young woman in a very short emerald dress. I was comforted to see that he had a full plate in hand to help him gain strength for the ordeal ahead.

A youngish gentleman in a fawn-colored suit and a truly wonderful tie had been eyeing Jackie hungrily for several minutes. Suddenly he wedged himself between Jackie and me and started talking. "That instrument you play," he said to her, "the viola-da-what's-it; does it take a long time to learn?"

"Well—"

"The reason I asked," the gentleman said, smoothly but a little hurriedly, "was because if it's pretty easy I thought maybe you could give me lessons. I mean, I've always wanted to play an instrument."

Good grief. When does he get around to hinting that maybe they could, heh heh, make beautiful music together?

"Well . . ." Jackie was blushing slightly.

"No, seriously. You do give lessons, don't you?"

I waited. It shouldn't take long for Jackie to recover her balance. It didn't. "I do indeed," she said demurely. "Would you want individual or group?"

"Oh, individual, definitely."

"That's wonderful," Jackie said, "I'd love it. My husband's just behind you. He can give you all the details."

"Oh. He is?"

" 'Fraid so," I said.

Fawn Suit turned to face me. He smiled weakly. "Oh. Well. Er, maybe I better call you."

"Fine," I said heartily, handing him one of our special Antiqua Players business cards with the lyre on it. "You can catch us at this number. Private lessons start at three hundred an hour."

"*Dollars?*"

"Ms. Craine is the world's leading gamba player," I said in a shocked voice. "Surely you wouldn't expect her to make herself available to a beginning pupil for less."

"No, I suppose not," the young man said. "Oh well. I just thought . . ."

"Of course," I said magnanimously. "Why don't you think it over some more and let us know?"

"Maybe I should. Thanks."

"Not at all. Bye," I said.

He backed away, still looking at Jackie like a kid in front of a candy counter, and headed for the bar.

"You always do that," Jackie complained.

"Do what?"

"Scare people off like that."

"Isn't that what you wanted me to do?" I asked her.

"Yes, in a way, but—"

"Come on, Jackie. That guy no more wants to take gamba lessons than he wants to learn Cajun cookery. The first thing, he shows up and he stops after about five minutes and says, 'While I'm resting, tell me all about *you*.' The second lesson, he suggests that maybe you'd like to come to his place for the third lesson. I'm not denying that his place is probably like the Taj Mahal. If you go, then comes the heavy, heavy action. If you don't, he never comes back."

"You know what?" Jackie said. "I think you're jealous."

"You bet your sweet little ass!" I said, surreptitiously patting the item in question.

"Alan!" But then she smiled at me and my heart melted. "It's nice that you're so jealous."

"Come on, you two!" It was Boyle, returned from his voyage. "Let's go get introduced!"

At the far end of the huge room, comfortable seats were grouped around a fireplace with a crackling log fire. A mixed group of seven or eight older people had taken refuge there. Boyle led us up to them. "Mother . . ." The way he addressed the slight, dark-eyed woman somehow combined Henderson Place formality with great affection. "May I introduce Jacqueline Craine and Alan French, of the quintet who played for us this evening? Jackie, Alan . . . my mother, Sarah Boyle."

I caught my breath.

The only word to describe Mrs. Boyle was enchanting. She must have been at least seventy, and she made absolutely no effort to hide it. Yet there was no grande dame pretentiousness about her. If she wore makeup, I couldn't tell. Her dress was plainly cut. The one piece of jewelery she wore, apart from a wedding ring, was a simple gold bracelet. She was not, and could never have been, beautiful. She was much better than that. I couldn't take my eyes off her.

Mrs. Boyle held out a hand to us. Her voice was as exquisite as the rest of her. "Dear Jerry, how nice! Miss Craine—or should it be Ms.? one is never sure any more—and Mr. French, you played so very well. I've always wondered why it is that the viola da gamba, with that marvelous silvery tone, was replaced by the cello. Can you tell me?"

"I don't think I can," Jackie started to say, but Mrs. Boyle interrupted with a smile.

"Please call me Sally, and I shall call you by your first names. I may, mayn't I? It's so much more practical than all the mistering and mizzing."

We both nodded. She could have called me anything.

"Now, do go on with what you were saying. And, Jerry . . ."

"Mother?" This time, Jeremiah Boyle's voice bore just the least trace, the barest hint, of exasperation held in check. I wasn't surprised. Good God, imagine growing up in this woman's shadow!

"See if you can get that nice Cyril to bring us some more champagne."

"Will do." And off he went.

I really don't recall the details of that conversation. I remember keen questions about the gamba, about our choice of music. I remember a wonderful story about a concert Mrs. Boyle had attended as a very young girl, where the dear duke had kept on falling asleep and the duchess had finally asked a footman to trickle ice water down the front of his stiff shirt. I remember thinking that Jackie and I were being sparkling, even brilliant. And I remember feeling something akin to anguish when Jeremiah Boyle said smilingly, "Mother, I promised to introduce Jackie and Alan to lots of people, and here you won't let them go."

There was none of that nonsense about thank you for spending so much time with an old lady. Sally Boyle simply smiled in her turn and held out her hand again. "Of course," she said, "you must be on your way. I've so enjoyed this. You're delightful, both of you. Truly. You must come see me. Good night."

I felt as if I'd been knighted.

Boyle took us in tow again, and in dizzying succession we met a small, wiry state senator who chaired the committee overseeing the arts giveaway program of his state; a judge who sat on the boards of one museum and one university, both with active concert programs; a very young woman in a very low-cut dress who was introduced as the community relations veep of an immense ad agency; and the cultural attaché of the Japanese delegation to the United Nations.

Every one of these people except the senator was flatteringly complimentary about our work. The lady veep asked when and where we'd be playing in public next, because she knew her boss, the senior vice president in charge of public affairs, would love to come. She didn't quite ask for comp tickets and I didn't offer her any.

The cultural attaché seemed to be inviting us to a reception at his embassy or legation or whatever it was called. I say "seemed" because it wasn't clear whether we were supposed to come as guests or to provide free musical entertainment.

Ralph, who had rejoined us, cut off what might have been an embarrassing question on my part and tactfully declined for us all on the grounds of a previous engagement.

"Some other time, maybe," the attaché said with an ambiguous smile and drifted off into the crowd.

Boyle's guests were beginning to slip away, which was a welcome sight. My feet were beginning to ache, my face felt stiff from smiling so much, and I could see that Jackie too was running out of steam. "Come on," I said to her, "let's pack up and go home."

We all wandered back to where we'd played and began the quiet little job of gathering up music, collapsing stands, and putting instruments into their cases. Ralph had already lowered the lid of his harpsichord and locked the case. His movers would pick it up the next morning.

Boyle himself broke away from his last few farewells and strolled over to watch the operation. With him was another man. "Here's one more person I want you to meet," he said to me. "Raymond Gerard, Alan French and Jackie Craine."

"Happy to meet you," the man said. We shook hands.

Gerard was about five nine and slender. I would have guessed he was in his late forties. He wore a well-tailored light gray business suit, a white shirt with a starched collar, and a maroon tie with an unobtrusive pattern. In fact, everything about him was unobtrusive. His spectacles, old-fashioned ones with thin silver rims, gave him a scholarly look, like a professor or perhaps an accountant, but the blue eyes behind them were sharp and watchful.

"Ray takes care of all sorts of things around here," said Boyle.

"Oh."

"One of the things he looks after is . . . arrangements. That right, Ray?"

"You could say so, I suppose." Ray's voice was low-pitched and polite, with a touch of Bronx Irish in it but not much deference, to Boyle or anybody else. "I guess what he's trying to do, Mr. French, is to get me to give you this." He reached into an inside pocket and handed me a sealed envelope.

"Wait a minute," I said. "We've already been paid."

"This is in addition to that," Boyle said. "And please don't say no."

"Oh," I said again, "well, I won't. Thanks very much."

"I thought you did a nice job," said Gerard.

"Come on, Ray, they were a lot better than that," Boyle protested.

I did the obvious thing and kept quiet, wondering about the relationship between the two men. Was Gerard some sort of privileged old Boyle family retainer to be able to talk like that? But I didn't have time to think more about it. Boyle was saying good night. "Ray will see to it that you're taken care of. I'm afraid I have to excuse myself. Things to do. But thanks. Thanks very much." And he was gone.

"Well now," Ray Gerard said, "are you all packed up?"

A few minutes later, laden with instruments and accessories, we followed him through the now empty house to the front entrance. He opened the door for us. The rain was still coming down. A huge black stretch limousine was waiting outside. Gerard motioned to the chauffeur, who got out and came across the sidewalk with a huge black umbrella.

"For us?"

"That's right," Gerard said. "Mr. Boyle insisted. John, help these people load their stuff. Then take them wherever they want to go."

Jackie remembered our manners. "Mr. Gerard?"

"Ray. Raymond if you want to be formal."

"Raymond, then. Tell Mr. Boyle thanks from all of us, won't you? And you too. Thanks for helping us."

"You're welcome, young lady. And maybe I was a little rude there a moment ago. I thought your music was enjoyable, very enjoyable indeed."

"It's nice of you to say so. Good night."

"Good night to you."

Boyle's limousine slithered across Eighty-sixth Street, up York Avenue, and then south on the FDR Drive. I thought I detected shocked disapproval in the set of John the chauffeur's shoulders when we first directed him all the way downtown to Jake the luthier's on Essex Street to drop off David, and then out to Queens for Terry, but it might have been my imagination.

On the way back to Manhattan, Jackie fell asleep with

her head on my shoulder. I was half asleep myself when something Ralph said suddenly snapped me wide awake.

"That Raymond Gerard is an interesting man."

"Yes he is. Is he Boyle's valet or what?"

"I haven't the faintest. But what I really don't understand . . ."

"Mmm?"

Ralph leaned closer and kept his voice low so John the chauffeur wouldn't hear. "Why would he be carrying a gun at a musicale? And a three-fifty-seven Magnum at that?"

I was so tired, I could only remember a tired old line. "Please don't shoot the piano player, he's doing the best he can."

CHAPTER 5

*T*he envelope from Boyle held a check for five hundred dollars. "Is there some moral issue involved? Does this violate our no tipping policy?" I asked deadpan. Nobody said a word. On the contrary, we all thought it was a lovely gesture. A hundred dollars of it went into the Antiqua Players checking account, chief signatory, Jackie, for contingencies like paying the phone bill. The rest we shared out evenly.

Ralph's eighty dollars bought him two more rare volumes of French harpsichord music and a new cedarwood litter box for Cat Frescobaldi.

David paid off a little more of his indenture to Jake and sent away to Venice for new strings for the chitarrone.

Terry put his money in the bank. He'd been doing that a lot lately. We wondered why, but Terry didn't tell us.

Jackie and I, after a couple of days of intense debate,

invested most of our Boyle bonus in fabric for new bedroom curtains.

It stopped raining for one day, the day Jackie went shopping for the fabric. Then it snowed. When it stopped snowing and began to rain again, New York was well supplied with that late winter essential, frozen slush, most of it caking our sidewalk and clogging the gutter in front of the entrance. Needless to say, Ramón the super was not available to deal with the slush. He was in Arizona for his health.

The next morning Jackie set up the sewing machine in the bedroom and went to work on the curtains. I began some sorely needed practice on the treble viol. The result of all of this diligence was that we nearly didn't hear the telephone when it rang.

I did hear it, though, and I sprinted to the kitchen to pick it up.

"That you, Mr. French?"

"Yes."

"Hold the wire for Mr. Boyle."

Huh?

"Alan French, Jeremiah Boyle here. You too busy to talk?"

"No, not at all," I said.

"Good. Now, listen. Some very nice friends of mine and I are chartering a yacht. We're going to be cruising from Key West out into the Caribbean for a day or two. What I want to know is, would you be available to go on the cruise and do a concert for us?"

I was flabbergasted. "You mean me personally or the Antiqua Players?"

"No, no, the Antiqua Players. You and Jackie and the whole nine yards. We'll fly you down there and back, of course."

A yacht. The Caribbean. Sunshine. Warmth.

"How soon would this be?" I asked cautiously.

"We'd be taking off next Tuesday. You'd probably be back, oh, in three or four days."

"Sounds fantastic," I said, "but I do have to check with the others."

"Well, tell them the fee would be the same as for the other night."

"Don't go away," I said fervently. "We'll call you right back."

Boyle chuckled. "Hell, you don't need me. Talk to Ray Gerard. He'll be making all the arrangements."

"I will," I vowed, "and thanks."

"Not at all. We'd love to have you," Boyle said cordially.

I put the receiver down and did another sprint into the bedroom to break the good news.

Five days later, suitcases and instruments in hand but still not quite believing, we sloshed our way across the apron at the LaGuardia general aviation facility and climbed aboard an unmarked jet headed for Miami.

"Holy wow!" Terry breathed. "We're not talking cabin cruiser, are we?"

I shook my head.

The onshore setting—thick clipped grass, beds of marigolds, flowering shrubs, pruned palm trees—was impressive enough. So was the small army of help, mostly Hispanic, that we could see keeping the grass clipped, the marigolds watered, the shrubs trimmed, the palms pruned, and interlopers on the far side of the ornate but businesslike iron fence that surrounded the place. But the most impressive spectacle was the flotilla of watercraft that snuggled up to the stone jetties and lay at moorings in the little bay.

Our yacht, by which I mean the one toward which the bronzed lad in the vaguely nautical getup was escorting us, was sparkling white, of course. Its two-deck superstructure made it as tall as a three-story house, and it must have been a hundred feet long. By the standards of this marina, that made it medium-size.

Two short aluminum and mahogany gangplanks were

rigged, one forward, one aft. As our guide led us past the aft one, I watched a sweating crewman wrestle three or four heavy crates up the slope to the main deck: cases of champagne.

"It's like the movies," Jackie said softly.

"Right," I said. "Me Cary, you Doris."

"I think you've got your genres mixed up," Ralph said. "This is definitely not a jungle." Of all of us, he was the only one dressed properly for the occasion, in a light blue linen blazer, striped polo shirt, white slacks, and rubber-soled canvas shoes.

We trooped up the main gangplank, to be greeted at the top by another tanned seafarer, a lean man with that ageless look professional outdoorsmen cultivate, no doubt because it gives them an edge over the indoorsmen they get paid to look after. He struck me as being in his midforties. "Welcome aboard *Enchantress*," he said pleasantly, sizing us up as useless in a storm or other marine crisis but taking due note of Jackie. "I'm Tom Hayward, the skipper."

As we introduced ourselves, Hayward unobtrusively checked our names against a list in a small notebook. Then he led us down a companionway to our cabins, which opened onto an interior corridor he called "the main deck," and showed us what switches worked what, how to ring for the steward, and how to undog the portholes.

"You'll want to unpack and wash up," he said in a soft drawl. "After that, you all just come on up one flight to the boat deck. We'll be serving drinks and you'll probably want to visit with Mr. Boyle and his friends before dinner." His voice was respectful enough, but his grin made me wonder. "There are some real interesting folks in the party."

With Jackie's gamba in one corner, our bags and my instruments in another, and a king-size bed in the middle, there was none too much room to spare in our cabin. But it had its own tiny bath and shower, soft carpeting on the floor—aboard this vessel, it seemed silly to call it the deck—and fresh roses in a vase on the dresser.

I finished unpacking first and sprawled on the bed while Jackie folded and unfolded, hung up and put away.

"I just hope I have enough clothes," she said worriedly.

"Relax," I said. "You're here to play, not compete with the audience, and when you're not playing you can hang around in a bathing suit. Besides . . ."

"Besides what?"

"I think it could be argued that you've got too *much* to wear, if anything. Come over here and let's see."

She came over to the bed and sat down beside me. "You don't want to be late for drinks, do you?"

"Certainly not," I said, reaching for her.

"Well, we will be," she said a little breathlessly a moment later.

"Will be what?"

"Mmm-m-m. Late for drinks."

"But I was right," I said after another not inactive moment.

Her murmur had a question mark at the end of it.

"You do have too much on."

"I *did* have, you mean. Alan . . ."

"Now what?"

"What if that captain came back and found us?"

"He'd be jealous," I said.

"No, really."

"Well, he would be. But I give up." Reluctantly, I released her, and she sat up and looked at me.

"You're sweet," she said suddenly, and swooped down to addle my wits with a long kiss. It took us several more minutes to disentangle ourselves, get off the bed, and render ourselves fit to be seen.

They'd set up a bar on the boat deck, with a crew-cut blond kid out of a surfer movie to hand out the cocktails and offer the hors d'oeuvres.

It was an idyllic scene, looking out over the harbor to the sea beyond, all glittering blue water and huge bright yachts. Idyllic but not altogether tranquil. When we arrived, two men were standing by the rail wrapped in intense conversation. One of them looked up and nodded, but the other barely noticed us. By the time we'd been given our drinks—I had a gin and tonic, Jackie a San Pellegrino—the conversation had erupted into into noisy argument.

"God damn it, what the whole Caribbean Basin needs is more of this," one of the men was proclaiming. He gestured with his empty glass at the harbor. "Tourism, tourism, and more tourism. That's the right way to aid these economies. We have to help them import tourists."

"I agree with you, Atley." The second man munched a prawn, licked the barbecue sauce from the corner of his mouth, and spun the toothpick overboard. "I agree, peaceful development is the ideal. But we have to be realistic. We have to be objective. Cuba was a tourist paradise, after all, under Batista. But we turned our backs on it for just a few months, we let it alone and bang! Castro. For a quarter of a century that bastard has been exporting revolution. And don't the Sovs love it."

"So the right thing to do is send in the Eighty-second Airborne and the gunships? Why, you're right out of the nineteenth century—no, make that the eighteenth."

"Now, Atley, you know I don't say that."

"He doesn't say that, A.R.," Jeremiah Boyle said soothingly in a tone of voice calculated to annoy. He winked at us mischievously.

"No, that's right," said the man Boyle had called A.R. "They don't say it in public where you can debate it. They *do* it when nobody's looking." His voice trailed off sullenly. "I need another drink."

"You certainly do," Boyle said. "And you need to meet these new people. You too, Everett."

"Oh, you boys," sighed a round-faced woman in a pink dress and a woolly gray sweater. "You're always fighting."

"No we're not, Charlotte." The man who wanted to be realistic and objective about the Caribbean gobbled another prawn and took a sip of his drink. "We're just having an exchange of views."

Oddly, his face was familiar. I knew I'd seen it somewhere before. I couldn't think where, but I knew I didn't care for the little smirk of satisfaction it wore as he turned away.

"Well, it sounded just like a fight to me," the woman said. "Atley, don't pay any attention to Everett when he starts talking like that."

The man called A.R. nodded. He took a deep pull of his drink. "Honey, you're a hundred percent right," he said amiably. He looked around to make sure the other man wouldn't be able to hear. "Arguing with Everett is like getting in a pissing contest with a skunk."

"A.R., Everett, my dear friends, I hear you both," Boyle said. "Calm yourselves and meet some people who I swear won't argue with you at all. In fact, they're dedicated to soft touches of sweet harmony."

"Shakespeare, *Merchant of Venice,* act five, scene one," A.R. said surprisingly. "And you must be the musicians who are going to play for us. Well, welcome aboard."

"This learned scholar is Atley R. Sensabaugh," Boyle told us. "And Charlotte here is Mrs. Sensabaugh."

We shook hands all around.

"Jerry," said a throaty voice behind us, "aren't you going to introduce me, too?" The voice belonged to a slim woman with a deep tan. Her black sundress might have been an inch too short for someone her age, but the legs it revealed were admirable, and there wasn't much wrong with the rest of her, either.

"But of course. Ladies and gentlemen," Boyle said with mock formality, "allow me to present Mrs. Everett Feuerman."

"Please, call me Kitty." She held out a hand to me with a friendly smile that wanted to reach her eyes.

I smiled back automatically and murmured something polite. I took notice of her clear-cut Nefertiti features and the gold earrings and gold necklace she wore, but I didn't pay much attention to what she was saying. I was too busy putting two and two together. No wonder Mr. Realistic and Objective looked so familiar. He was Everett Feuerman, and he was famous. Everett Feuerman had been a hotshot in the State Department, assistant secretary or under secretary or something for Latin America, and a year ago—was it only a year ago?—he'd fired off a mighty blast in a Senate hearing against U.S. policy and resigned and gone on all the talk shows. Then he'd signed up with some Wall Street firm for a fabulous salary, and *that* made the evening news. And here he was on Boyle's boat, eating prawns and arguing and being a love and fetching his wife a drink.

"You're the same people who played at Jerry's party last month, am I right?"

What persuades paunchy people to wear those horizontally striped, long-sleeved knit shirts that betray their every bulge? And what makes them go in for light blue denim shorts with white belts? Everett Feuerman dressed for play certainly didn't look like a sharp young ex–under secretary of state or hard-hitting investment banker. He looked podgy and tired and older than his years. Behind his thick horn-rims his brown eyes were wary. But his manner was well on the far side of assertive.

I admitted that we were who we were.

Feuerman was on me like a cat. "I'm Everett Feuerman. You know, I wondered at the time what made you screw up that one piece before your break."

"It was all my fault. I wrote a dumb arrangement."

He brushed aside my feeble attempt to be disarming. "Well, I certainly hope you don't do it again. You want people to listen to you, don't you? When I'm listening, I hate mistakes. They absolutely destroy my concentration."

Good grief.

But just when I was about to counter with something equally offensive, Feuerman turned to Jackie and smiled, showing a great many teeth. "I didn't have any problem with *your* playing, though," he said. "It was very strong. Very wonderful. Marais, that's difficult music. No wonder he's neglected. Have you ever thought of doing a Marais record?"

"Yes, but—"

"I know, don't tell me. There's no real market for it. When I was a young man, I wanted to start my own record company just to do things that the big companies wouldn't do. Like your kind of music."

"What happened?" I asked him.

"Oh, well," he said vaguely, "young people get funny ideas. It wouldn't have worked. Not big enough. Art is never big enough. If you want to set up a market-oriented business in the entertainment field, you have to think in terms of substantial dollar intake. You can't do that in the arts."

"I see," I said, my dreams of setting up a market-oriented business in the entertainment field shattered forever.

"Well, anyway, good to meet you. You, too, pussycat." He couldn't resist a parting shot at me. "Hope you do better tomorrow night than you did last time." Feuerman turned away, hunching his shoulders as if we were reporters asking him unpleasant questions, and buttonholed a tall man in a salmon pink cotton sweater. "Tommy," I heard him say, "you're going to have to change . . ." But what Tommy was going to have to change, whether it was his foreign policy, his brand of Scotch, or his spots, I wasn't able to tell.

Jackie was opening her mouth to tell me what she thought of a former under secretary of state who called her "pussycat" when Ray Gerard came up to us.

"Mr. French. Miss Craine." Gerard was wearing a kelly green blazer and tan slacks with the crease in them so sharply defined that the material looked like folded paper. Was he carrying his gun? I couldn't tell, but he *was* carrying a big Polaroid camera, one of the early models, its strap slung around his neck. "You want to just stand apart for a minute while I get you? . . . Good, that's good. Okay, now, one more . . . good. Thanks." He snapped the shutter a second time, pulled out the developing print, and put it in his blazer pocket with the first print.

"What's this all about?" I asked. "I don't see you as a photographer."

"Nah, it's not for me," Gerard said. "It's for taxes."

"What do you mean?"

"Everybody on the boat, I have to take their picture. That way, we have a record, who was there. Malcolm Forbes told Jerry he's done it for years on the *Highlander*. Goes in the guest book with the date and your signature. So the feds can see it's a business trip."

"A *business* trip?"

Gerard looked a little discomfited, as if he'd said too much and knew it. "Well, sure, for tax reasons."

I looked at Jackie and shrugged. For us the cruise *was* a business trip; what Boyle called it was his own affair. And his tax man's, of course.

"Anyway, you want a shot of the two of you together?" Gerard asked. "I've got all the film in the world. Okay, just move over by the rail and stand close. A little closer. Good enough." He handed us the developed print with a cheerful wink. "Pretty nice shot, if I say so myself."

It was, as a matter of fact.

He'd caught Jackie in the act of smiling her wonderful smile, while I was looking unusually serious, not to say dour. But the best thing about the picture was the large, the very large, seagull that Gerard had somehow caught in mid flight. It was about five feet away, its beak was open hungrily, and it looked as if it was going to land on my left shoulder.

Boyle came up to us just as Gerard drifted away. "Let's see it," he said, holding out a sinewy hand for the print. He laughed at the gull. "Who's that, your muse? Calliope, she must be. Please. I must show this to someone. Mother . . ."

"Surely not," said a cool familiar voice. "Surely their muse would be Euterpe. Euterpe looks after lyric song. Calliope is the muse of epic verse. You should know that, Jerry."

My heart skipped a beat. Jackie took a look at my face, smiled, and squeezed my hand. She understood.

Sally Boyle on board a yacht was at least as devastating as Sally Boyle in a New York town house. A huge straw hat kept the afternoon sun off her face. A gay scarf went over the crown and floppy brim, tied under her chin to keep the sea breeze from blowing the hat away.

"You know," I blurted, "I'd like to paint you like that." I don't think I've ever said anything so absurd to anyone in my life, but Mrs. Boyle didn't seem to mind at all. On the contrary, her lips twitched in a reminiscent smile.

"When I was a very young girl in Paris, Mr. Pascin said precisely the same thing to me. Of course . . ." She paused, gauging our reaction and picking her moment. "He was a *terrible* man. In his next breath he suggested that we do something very naughty together."

I yearned to ask whether she'd done it, but I didn't dare.

"It's so *good* to see you and Jackie again," Mrs. Boyle went on. She said it as if the three of us were friends who had known and loved each other since childhood. It was only her good manners, but it made me wish it were true.

"Alan talks about you all the time," Jackie said. "He says there are no other women in the world besides you."

Mrs. Boyle twinkled at Jackie. I'm sorry, that's what she did; there's no other way to express it. "How charming of him. I'd best be careful, then. Shipboard flirtations can be dangerous, you know. But heavens, instead of all this silly talk, tell me what you've decided to play for us. And please, can I meet your other friends?"

A sudden startling blast of sound interrupted her. It was the yacht's foghorn. While we'd been talking, the crew had cast off the mooring lines. I hadn't heard the engines start or noticed when we'd begun to move, but we had already edged away from shore and picked up headway as we started toward the harbor entrance. Everything looked beautiful and a little unreal, gilded by the sun.

Jackie stood beside me at the rail and squeezed my hand

again. And I remember what Sally Boyle said then. In fact, I can almost hear her say it. Her exact words were, "It's always exciting, isn't it, the start of a voyage? Even a tiny little one is an adventure."

CHAPTER 6

The weather the next morning came straight out of a travel spectacular. *Enchantress* was living up to her name.

We took our seconds of breakfast coffee and rolls out on deck and watched with awe as a rocky headland emerged gleaming from the sea mist off our starboard bow. "Andros," somebody said.

Up on the bridge, the huge chart spread out on the map table showed us where Andros was, and the skipper's forefinger traced our progress, from the Florida Keys roughly eastward over the tip of the Bahaman Bank to where we were now. Once we rounded Andros, Hayward the skipper said, we'd be moving southward into Tongue of the Ocean. But when we asked him where we were headed after that, Hayward just grinned and shook his head. "That's up to the boss," he said, "and he hasn't told me yet."

Boyle wasn't around to ask, and neither were any of his

pals, so we all had a third cup of coffee and went on exploring the yacht. Actually, we were looking for the harpsichord Boyle had promised to have ready for us. We found it in the salon, a spacious seagoing living room with a bar at the bow end and, at the stern, paneled double doors opening onto an expanse of deck gleaming with varnish, the fantail.

The harpsichord wasn't a large one. It had only one manual, or keyboard, and two sets of strings, but its case was an elegant confection in antiqued white and gold. "Meant to look Venetian," Ralph said with a sniff. "Let's hope it sounds more Flemish." He dragged a chair up to the keyboard.

"It's only ten o'clock. Maybe you ought to wait," I said.

"Don't be a silly," said Sally Boyle from the doorway. "You play as much as you want. I was just hoping I'd find you all here." This morning, she was wearing a blouse and skirt and espadrilles. Her hair was pinned back behind her ears like Jackie's, to keep it out of the way. She looked as cheerful as a bluebird.

The most remarkable thing about her, I decided, was the way she moved. Her walk wasn't an old lady's hesitant walk, it was brisk like a dancer's or a young girl's. Aches and pains there may have been, but you were not to know it. I marveled at the discipline that had kept those muscles active for so many years and that back so straight.

Book in hand, Sally Boyle sat quietly on one of the sofas while Ralph fooled with the harpsichord. It took him about five minutes to figure out its registration and stops and test its playability. It sounded fine. "I'll have to touch it up later," he said, meaning retune it. "But it will do. It will more than do."

"Thank God." I breathed easier. Force Ralph to use a badly voiced or ill-maintained instrument and you risk a truly remarkable outburst of artistic temperament.

"Good morning, everyone. Good morning, Mother." Boyle, too, had on no-nonsense cruise clothes: khaki shorts, white button-down shirt with the sleeves rolled partway up his lean forearms, no socks, tan deck shoes. Aviator-type sunglasses dangled from his shirt pocket. "Good, you found the instrument. It's a nice one. Nice enough for shipboard, anyway." He drank from a big mug of hot tea. "Say, listen. What I thought we'd do is cruise until about six bells. That's four o'clock. Then we'll pull into one of those little bays on Exuma, anchor, maybe go for a quiet swim. A few more people will probably be turning up around drink time. Then if it's okay with you we'll all sit right out here on the poop at sunset and you can play for us."

"Sounds lovely," said Jackie.

We trooped out onto the fantail to look around. A smart breeze snapped the Royal Keys Yacht Club pennon like a firecracker and banged the brass fittings of its halyard sharply against its metal flagstaff.

"What about this wind? What about waves?" asked Alan French the landlubber and spoilsport.

"Won't be a problem this evening. Skipper will anchor us out of any wind and it'll be dead calm where we are, I guarantee it."

Whatever Boyle guaranteed, playing outdoors is always tricky for a chamber group. There's almost never no wind. We'd have to weight our music stands with something, and we'd need the spring clothespins Jackie had tucked into my bag to hold the music in place.

"There's not going to be a reggae band cutting loose on shore, is there?" I asked anxiously. Sound carries for miles over water, and all we needed was competition from four or five steel drums and a squadron of electric guitars.

Boyle looked at me a little impatiently. "I give you my absolute word there will be nothing like that."

"Bugs?"

The impatience was rapidly ripening into irritation. "There won't *be* any bugs. We'll be too far offshore."

"Really, Jerry," Sally Boyle said. "These are perfectly sensible questions. The least you can do is be polite."

"Sorry, Mother. Sorry, Alan," Boyle said at once. "Didn't

mean to sound uncivil. But where we'll be anchored the little devils won't come after us."

"Fair enough," I capitulated.

"If you're really worried about it, we can spray," Boyle said.

"The only thing I'm really worried about," I said, "is finding someplace to rehearse where you won't be listening to the entire program ahead of time."

"Easiest thing in the world," Boyle said. "Use this room right here. We'll all go up on the boat deck and stay there until you're done. You won't bother us and we won't bother you. And after that we can have some fun."

"In that case, let's set up and rehearse," I said. "There's no time like the present, I always say."

"You've never said that before in your entire life," Jackie said a few minutes later, carrying her gamba over to a seat and skillfully wriggling past my instrument bag and the two music stands I'd brought in from the cabin.

"Shh," I said. "We have to think of our image."

"Which reminds me," Ralph said, "how do we dress for tonight?"

"Jackie?"

"Navy dress whites with the high collar, white buck shoes—"

"Okay, admiral, what should we wear really?"

We settled on our usual summer uniform of blouse and long skirt for Jackie and dark slacks and white shirts for the males. "If it gets chilly," I said. "we'll stop and put on sweaters."

"I didn't bring my sweater," said David. "I left it at—" He automatically looked around to make sure she wasn't listening. "You know, at Simone's," he finished, lowering his voice.

"If we could just take the Schein from bar twenty-seven of the intrada," I said patiently.

"It's okay, David," Jackie said, "I packed one for you."

"Bar twenty-seven—what do you mean, you packed one for him?"

"It's not your silk and cotton Christmas one," Jackie explained. "It's the old navy wool one that you keep saying you want to get rid of."

"I never."

"Now, now," she soothed. "You wouldn't want David to catch cold, would you?"

"Please, everybody," I whimpered. "Bar twenty-seven. One, two, three and four and go!"

We knew the music well, so the rehearsal was really only a run-through. An hour later, I called it a morning and we put away our gear and hurried out into the sunshine.

Charlotte Sensabaugh was standing by the rail. I wouldn't want to say that she was exactly lying in wait, but at dinner the night before she'd grilled me on the subject of the musical life, which she simply adored, and she did have that expectant look on her face. "Alan! and Miss Craine! Isn't this the most terrific weather! It should be perfect for our little concert. Now, tell me the truth about Jean-Pierre Rampal."

"I don't *know* the truth about Jean-Pierre Rampal, Charlotte," I confessed, "except what I read in the reviews."

"Oh, well, never mind, I thought you might be a friend of his. Jerry knows him."

"He does?" I was wondering whether we could promote ourselves a prelunch coffee.

"Well, Jerry knows everybody. I mean, look at the people on this boat." Boat! I shuddered. *Enchantress*'s skipper would keelhaul her if he heard her say that, but Charlotte kept right on going. "There's Everett, and there's Tommy, that's what they call him but his real name's Robin, Robin Williamson, he's vice chairman of New York National"—so that's who Tommy was—"and his wife's name is Victoria, in case you haven't met her yet, but we call her Tory. And I guess Hugh Shaver will be coming later and bringing that girlfriend of his, Christine Cowper—"

"Hey, wait a minute," I said, "I think I need a scorecard."

"—and Kitty, Jerry knows Kitty like . . . something. Like the palm of his hand."

Jackie and I looked at each other wonderingly.

"Goodness gracious, my dears, it's common knowledge. They've been lovers for years."

I found my voice. "And, er, Everett?"

"Oh, Everett knows, of course. And he seems not to mind, poor thing, though it may be that he's just so busy that he hasn't got time to mind. But I sometimes think that's why he's so argumentative."

"How do you know all this?" I asked her.

"Kitty and I were roommates at Smith," she said.

Fascinating. "And Smith roommates tell each other everything?"

"Exactly. At least, we always do. Poor Kitty."

"Why poor Kitty?"

"She puts up with so much. She swears it's worth it, but my golly, you have to wonder. Just the other day, it came out about Jerry and Lauren."

"Lauren?"

Charlotte pursed her lips in obvious disapproval. "Oh, you'll be meeting her soon enough. She's flying down to join us, or so I'm told. Lauren Winship. She's an economist. She's terribly, terribly brainy. And terribly, terribly attractive. At least, some people think so. Oh, hello, Jerry."

"What, are you talking about Lauren again?" Boyle ambled up and flashed us his leprechaun grin. He'd clearly heard every word Charlotte had said, but if it made him uncomfortable he gave no sign. "Lauren is definitely not one of Charlotte's favorite people, is she, Charlotte?"

"Now, Jerry, don't put words in my mouth."

"Far be it from me to do any such thing. But Lauren Winship? You've heard of the Winship Cycle? Well, no, you wouldn't have, it's a rather technical bit of economic analysis. But let me tell you the real truth about Lauren Winship. Her swimsuits reverse the law of supply and demand."

Charlotte bit. "What on earth are you talking about?"

"The more there is of Lauren, the more the demand," Boyle answered over his shoulder as he walked away.

"We'll just pretend we didn't hear that, won't we?" Charlotte said to us too brightly. "And that reminds me, my twelve-year-old wants to change flute teachers. You must know someone, we're in the Chicago area . . ."

It took several minutes to convince her that even though I play the flute I don't keep a register of all the flautists in the world, and that even though her daughter Cecily is a budding genius I wouldn't consider moving to Chicago to offer her instruction. After that our relationship grew slightly more distant. Eventually Charlotte decided that she was getting too much sun and went back to her cabin.

"My Lord!" Jackie said.

"Don't worry," I said, squeezing her. "Nothing like that can ever happen to us."

"How can you be so sure?"

"For one thing, you didn't go to Smith, you went to Oberlin. For another . . ."

"Yes?"

"Our daughter, whenever we have her, already has a flute teacher."

"Oh, darling," said Jackie, "you've signed her up with Jean-Pierre Rampal."

"Hello, you two. Signed who up?" Boyle was back. We explained and he laughed. Then he said abruptly, "Say, Jackie, come for a little walk with me. There's something I want to talk to you about." Before I could object, he put his arm around her shoulders and swept her down the deck in the direction of the bow.

I was a bit nonplussed, but what the hell? If Boyle wanted to behave like a coxcomb this lovely morning, I could bear it. Maybe he was just hungry. So I shrugged it off and looked out at the sea and the sky and soaked up some of that wonderful Caribbean warmth. And a few minutes later Ralph came up to me with a question about one of the pieces in the program and we got into a discussion and I more or less forgot about Boyle's having taken Jackie off somewhere until Jackie herself came marching up the deck toward us. Alone.

Ralph took one look at her and, tactful chap, slipped away to look over his music.

"What's wrong?" I said.

She shook her head, meaning that she didn't want to talk where people might overhear, grabbed me, and propelled us both below to our cabin. She sat on the bed and looked up at me. "I've just been . . . assaulted."

"What?"

"Oh, don't worry," she said shakily. "My virtue is intact. But that so-and-so . . ." She went limp for a moment and I sat down next to her and just held her. Then she caught her breath. *"Christus!* I was actually scared. He's very strong, you know. And he's . . . ungovernable. Almost."

I heard myself saying in a kind of frantic calm, "Wait a minute, wait a minute. It's okay. You're okay. Just tell me what happened."

She shook her head again. "I'm sorry to be so upset," she said. "It was ridiculous, but he . . ."

"Tell me," I prompted.

"Well, you saw him grab me and parade me along the deck."

"Yes. I didn't like it much but I didn't see any real harm in it. I figured the guy had on his macho suit and was just showing off."

Jackie bit her lip. "It was worse than that. He sort of whisked me to where the deck curves around the front of the ship. It's windy there, so nobody was around. He kept on holding me with one arm and he pointed over the side with the other, and it was a school of porpoises or dolphins and they were beautiful. They'd spout and dive and spout and dive and the spray would go up in the air and sparkle in the sun, and that was really exciting. But all the time he was holding me and I was watching . . ."

"Go on."

"I suddenly realized he was talking away a mile a

minute. About how talented I was and how talented women really turned him on and how talent made its own rules and not to worry about the consequences because for people like us there were no consequences."

"Yuck," I said.

"Then he made his big move and tried to kiss me."

"And you did what?"

"I pushed him away, of course. And I told him that I'd made up my own mind long ago about who I wanted and that it was you."

I held her closer. "What did he say to that?"

"He sort of backed off without quite letting go and said he understood. But when I changed my mind—not if, 'when'—I would remember what he'd said and I would call him. Alan, he wasn't a bit embarrassed. He was just oozing conceit. Grr!"

"But *you* were embarrassed," I said.

She buried her face against my shoulder for a second. "You're right. I was mortified. He even gave me his card with his unlisted number, for when I was ready. Can you imagine? Here." She fished it out of the pocket of her shorts and handed it to me.

I was so angry I was scarcely coherent. "Listen. Just say the word and I'll tell Boyle to shove this concert right up his ass."

Jackie made a sound halfway between a sob and a giggle. "I know you would, darling, but please don't."

"Why?"

"Don't you see? He wouldn't care. He'd just smile and say that it's too bad how narrow-minded some people are, and how he thought you'd be more of a man of the world than that."

"Wouldn't he have to say *something* to his guests?"

"Oh, he'd make up some story. He might even tell them . . ."

"I know what you're thinking," I said. "He'll say that

you'd gone after *him*. After all, actresses and musicians. Okay, what do you want to do?"

"Wash my face," she said promptly. "It's dumb, but I really do feel dirty. And then spend the afternoon with you and play a terrific concert as if nothing had happened."

"Are you really up to playing?"

"Not right now," she admitted. "But I will be."

"And you don't want me to do anything to the son of a bitch?"

"Please. For me. Don't."

"All right. But we have to tell the others."

She nodded. One of the few Antiqua Players ground rules is that anybody who's upset immediately before a concert has to tell the rest of us out loud what's wrong. When one of us is troubled, it's bound to affect our performance, but at least if we know in advance we can watch out for lapses and try to cover them or make up for them.

I left Jackie to wash up and went back to the boat deck. Fortunately, there was no sign of Boyle. I had to interrupt a spirited game of hearts to do it, but I collected the others and gathered them below. Jackie explained. The reactions came as absolutely no surprise.

"What a sleazebag," Terry said. "We should feed him to the fishes like in *The Godfather*."

"Yeah," said David, "but maybe you brought it on yourself a little bit by going around in those shorts."

"What do you think I should wear in this weather," Jackie retorted sweetly, "a long black overcoat?"

"The man's a sex-and-power sickie, all right," Ralph said, "but there's no way he can hurt *you*."

Jackie's eyes filled with tears. "That's sweet, Ralph. Thank you."

We all agreed that playing well would be the best revenge, especially if we could eat well and drink well into the bargain. Our timing was perfect. No sooner had we made this decision than the gong sounded for lunch.

CHAPTER 7

despicable lecher Boyle may have been, but fair is fair, he was also an incomparable host. He lunched us on fresh seafood Newburg washed down with a really remarkable wine, I think a Moselle. His table talk was, as they say, scintillating. He gave us two hours in which to recover. And at four o'clock exactly, *Enchantress* dropped anchor in a deserted cove that looked like yet another ad for a holiday paradise and all hands were invited to turn out for a swim.

While we were changing, I suggested to Jackie that instead of her bikini she might prefer something a little less provocative, like a gunnysack.

My remarks were less than favorably received. "You're as bad as David. The water looks heavenly, but because the great Jeremiah Boyle might say or do something, you want me to wrap myself up like the women in Iran. No way. Besides, my gunnysack takes too long to dry."

Any doubts I had about Jackie's morale promptly vanished.

Boyle the lecher wasn't ready to give up. He was right there in bathing suit and sunglasses, a yachtsman's peaked cap tilted elegantly over one eye, as Jackie, not sparing him a glance, walked barefoot by him. "Gadzooks, what a beautiful woman!" He said it to me facetiously, but Jackie was meant to overhear.

"I take it you're speaking strictly as a connoisseur," I said.

He looked at me, startled, and raised his eyebrows. I could have laughed out loud. It hadn't occurred to him until then, I suppose, that Jackie might have talked over their little encounter with her husband. In Boyle's circle, that didn't happen. Finally, he said, "My dear Alan, of course. But she *is* exquisite."

"She can swim, too," I said.

Jackie draped her towel over the rail, stepped onto the tiny stage they'd rigged for swimming, and split the water ten feet below in a graceful dive. A few seconds later, much less gracefully, I joined her. Before long, most of the party was in the water. It was fun to watch. Feuerman swam industriously back and forth between two imaginary markers, bumping into people but getting his exercise. Sensabaugh kept doing surface dives, coming up for air with splashings and puffings like an overweight grampus. Kitty Feuerman, svelte in her black swimsuit and white cap, breaststroked sedately near the yacht and well within sight of Boyle. From time to time she glanced over at us. Had she guessed that Boyle had made what my mother would have called "advances" to Jackie?

Boyle himself was an interesting study. Bare-chested and suntanned, a can of what looked like tomato juice in one hand and a huge cigar in the other, he was the very model of an outdoors type. He shouted encouragement to newcomers on deck, he exchanged quips with those already swimming. But never once did he make any effort to go in the water.

Jackie, treading water, pushed her hair out of her eyes and giggled. "Here comes David."

When I looked, I laughed myself. David was balancing on the diving stage, ready to take the plunge. Cradled in his arms was an immense inflated rubber duckie. When I say immense, I'm not kidding. The thing was at least as long as he was tall. Its head and tail were attached to a pink circular tube that would have fit nicely inside the rear tire of a bulldozer. But the best thing about the float was that the hat on its head was cocked at exactly the same angle as the one Boyle was wearing.

Boyle was grinning, rather a sour grin, I thought. Maybe he too had spotted the resemblance.

With utmost seriousness, David leaned over and plopped the duckie into the water. Then he jumped in after it, climbed aboard, and arranged himself comfortably in the tube to laughter and applause.

"What do you say we dump him?" I asked.

"Better not," Jackie said. "Somebody might get hurt."

"Yeah," David said, "me."

He paddled away unscathed and Jackie decided to swim the width of the cove. I turned over on my back and let myself drift lazily toward shore. I had the vague idea that I'd stretch out on the beach and snooze until the heat of the sun drove me back in the water. Maybe if I signaled to Jackie, she'd join me.

The sound of voices roused me from my reverie. At the same instant, my submerged rear bumped against sand. But some instinct kept me from sitting all the way up. Instead, I raised my head a few inches and took a quick look around.

Feuerman and Sensabaugh were having at each other all over again. They had no idea anybody was within earshot, and they seemed oblivious to the fact that they were up to their navels in the Caribbean and that their hairy upper halves were starting to turn pink from the sun. Their focus was exclusively on each other, and they weren't arguing global politics.

As for me, what else could I do but lie there in a foot and a half of nice warm salt water and listen?

"Everett, will you stop being such a stubborn asshole?" Sensabaugh was saying. "You know we have to buy Cousin Sam Swain's fucking convertible preferred. You know we fucking well have to."

"I know no such thing," Feuerman shot back. He was less vehement, but even so he sounded like someone whose patience had run out. "If we make the right offer for the common and we do it fast enough, we don't have to worry about Samuel Swain *or* his preferred. And one other thing, Atley. I really don't care for some of your less pleasant speech habits, and neither do some other people I could mention. I'd suggest you clean up your act. Before it's too late."

Sensabaugh, red as a sunburnt beet, started to answer back, but just then Feuerman caught sight of me in my wallow. Immediately, he grabbed Sensabaugh by the arm to shut him up. They lowered their voices and turned away, and I lost what was said next.

A little guiltily, I waded out toward Jackie.

"What's wrong?" she said when she saw my face.

"Nothing, really. Those two characters were fighting over some sort of a deal. I don't think they like each other very much."

"A deal? I thought this was supposed to be a fun trip."

"Maybe deals are their fun. Anyway, it's not our problem. You want to go sit on the beach?"

"Oh, Alan, I can't. I have to get back to the yacht and practice and press my skirt and wash my hair. But give me a hug instead."

"Puritan," I said.

"Oh, no," she said in my arms. "Not that. Never that."

Boyle had told us that a few extra people would be dropping in to hear us play, but he hadn't mentioned how or when they'd be doing the dropping. So when the little seaplane buzzed by overhead, I didn't even look up.

"Hey," Terry said, "it's landing."

Moments later, it came taxiing up toward *Enchantress*. Its engine slowed and stopped and its three passengers came rowing across to us in a small rubber raft. Boyle was at the rail to kiss the pretty young arrival and exchange backslaps and growly pleasantries with the two men escorting her.

While this was happening, a white launch chugged into the cove and made fast alongside. Boyle left his first guests to welcome half a dozen new brightly clad visitors.

Finally, a two-masted sailboat glided in under power and dropped anchor, and yet another cluster of expensive-looking seafarers of both sexes clambered up a companion ladder from their dinghy to join the festivities. Everybody seemed to know everybody else, and there was much kissing of cheeks and mutual gripping of biceps and clinking of ice and pouring to keep things cheery.

"Gee," Jackie said, "all for us."

Ray Gerard, once again in the green blazer with the special pocket for spare bullets, came by to see how we were making out.

"We're fine," I said. "Those sandbags of yours are really terrific."

Early that morning, he'd sent a crewman ashore with half a dozen of the yacht's linen pillowcases. These, half filled with sand from the beach, were now draped over the legs of our music stands, to hold them down in a gale. Though the chances of a gale, I was happy to note, looked very slim indeed.

We'd already moved the harpsichord out of the salon and set it in place on the fantail, and Ralph had tuned it. We weren't using it in the first part of the concert, so all it would need—we hoped—was a once-over-lightly at the end of the intermission.

Gerard checked his watch. "Seven fifteen. The sun sets in about half an hour. The boss would like you to start just about then. We'll get the people seated. If that's okay with you, I mean."

"We'll be all set. But try to get people to leave their drinks. All that ice rattling . . ."

"Oh yeah," Gerard said. "We never thought of that. You're right, it would be noisy. Intrusive. Okay, we'll get them to check their booze for a while. Now, how about you? Can I send you up a platter of hors d'oeuvres?"

"No thanks," I said.

"Aw, come *on*," David said reproachfully.

"All right," I said. "Send up a plate of hors d'oeuvres, not a platter, for this young man."

We couldn't think of anything else we wanted, so Gerard sauntered off and we all went inside.

Jackie had to go back to our cabin to change into her concert togs. Terry and David, panic-stricken as always, rummaged through a cupboard, found a set of Chinese checkers, and started a game. David's hors d'oeuvres disappeared like snow in May. Ralph crept silently off to the john, came back, and lay down on a sofa. I offered him ginger ale but he just shook his head. He was wearing his mittens. All I could do was leave him to his misery.

Every musician warms up in his or her own fashion. Mine is to sit down in a corner and devote myself to imagining that the concert is *over* and that we've committed every ghastly mistake in the book. For some reason, this gloomy fantasy always makes me feel better.

Jackie came back in the room and made me feel better still. For this occasion, she'd gone strapless. The sun had tinted her skin a very faint rose and she'd been careful not to incur dreaded strap marks. Her bare white knit top and dark print skirt made a distinct impression. Terry and David actually stopped playing to look her over.

"You like it?" she asked.

"We like it," I answered. "The men will drool, the women will make acid remarks, and we'll have to chain Boyle to the wall."

The door from the deck opened. "We're getting the good

people seated right now," Ray Gerard said. "So whenever you're ready." He went out again.

We stood together near the door. Ralph sat up and came over to join us. You could see every freckle on his face.

I peered through the window in the door at the situation outside. "Better give it another minute or two."

We waited.

"Okay," I said, "let's tune. If we do it now, we can come on and play right away and kind of hit them by surprise. Terry, blow me an A." We could tune indoors because the first piece was scored for two recorders, treble viol, lute, and gamba, so we didn't have to worry about being in tune with the harpsichord.

"Good enough," I said when it was good enough. "We're on. The usual order. Jackie first, then David, then Ralph, then Terry, then me."

"Do we need the beat for the opening?" somebody asked.

"And three and four and *play*," I said.

Counting silently to ourselves, we opened the door and filed out into the placid air.

The evening was so beautiful it was almost ridiculous. The sun was beginning to set over the ridgeline of the cay to our right, yet the light was still bright even on those parts of the cove that were in shadow, lingering on it like a child reluctant to head homeward at the end of the day. The merest breeze ruffled the surface of the water. The scrape of a chair as we took our places was as startling as a gunshot, but the profound quiet prevailed over it immediately.

To complete the perfection, only music was wanting. And we supplied it.

I made a small pinching gesture with my fingers to signify *keep it down* and Ralph murmured *"Dolce, dolce,"* and we played.

Our opening was perfect. The music wasn't there and then it was; and there was no point at all at which you could say, they began. We don't get it that way very often. I remember thinking wryly that if only Boyle had invited the critics that evening we'd be world famous by morning.

Then, of course, we were too busy with Johann Hermann Schein and his Banchetto Musicale of 1617 to be conscious of what was going on. But a few things stick in my memory. Terry's face, usually so animated, looking almost dreamy above his fingers and the polished wood of his recorder. Our sound. In fact, that's what everyone remembered, how centered our sound was and how gently we played and how entirely Schein's little dances accorded with the setting sun, the soft blue sky, and the shadows shimmering on the water.

At the end the audience, Boyle's vain, fussy friends, heaven bless them, didn't make one single solitary sound.

Before they stopped being transfixed and became merely polite, I held up my hand for silence. In no more time than it took for Terry to swap his recorder for a flute and for me to drop my viol and snatch my violin, we were playing again. And not little dances but Arcangelo Corelli, two sonatas da camera played end to end that sounded as if God himself had decided to include them in the program.

Corelli's sonatas: open harmonies, two upper voices moving calmly over a bass that sometimes picks up a bar or two of melody on its own. The bass is mostly the gamba, with only touches of the lute. They're deceptively gentle, the sonatas, deceptively simple. To play them is to dance on the highest and most exposed of high wires.

Midway through the prelude of the first one, the one in G minor, I gazed over at Jackie. I saw my face mirrored in her eyes. Jackie looked back at me and we both smiled, and Terry nodded and waggled his eyebrows without breaking rhythm and David's lips were pursed in concentration or he would have smiled too. Terry was absolutely secure on the baroque flute as he had never been before that night, with never a flat or watery note, and Jackie was Jackie and the four of us made music. And in the corrente of the A major sonata we really lost ourselves. We forgot the audience, except that it too was somehow caught up in what we were doing, forgot our surroundings and just *poured* Corelli into the quiet like a libation to the nameless local gods of Boyle's Bahamian cay.

My shirt was soaked, my forehead was dripping, and my fingers were tacky on the fingerboard when we finished.

The sun was behind the hill. The whole cove was in shadow. A woman in the third row was weeping, trying to hold it back and dabbing at her eye makeup with a tiny handkerchief, while her escort sat clapping furiously, wearing an embarrassed grin.

I have no idea how we got ourselves off for intermission.

"Well, my dears," Ralph said. We were back in the salon. "It moved. The earth definitely moved. I felt it and I wasn't even playing, just turning pages."

Jackie hugged me hard.

"Seriously . . ." I began.

"Did anybody see my swab?" Terry demanded.

"Seriously—"

"Who stole it? I've got to swab out this flute."

"Who ate the last two salmon wedges?" That, needless to say, was David.

"SERIOUSLY, damn it!" I roared. Everybody stopped chattering and looked at me with mild curiosity. "I may be prejudiced," I said, "but it's quite possible that that's the best we've ever played and, well, it was great and thank you," I ended stirringly.

"That's all very well," Ralph said, "but you better change your shirt, otherwise you'll be sneezing all through the second half."

So much for my forceful dynamic leadership.

I did change, and Terry found his swab and dried out his flute and fetched the glass of water with the oboe reeds soaking in it and Boyle himself came by with Ray Gerard to see if we were ready.

"We'll never beat the first half," I said to the others as we lined up to go back out. "So let's not even try."

And that tells you how smart I am.

The Handel trio sonata we were playing next is an

odd-shaped work. It has five movements instead of the usual three, and it ends with two allegros, one right after the other. But it's filled with genial Handelian melodies, it's technically easy, and it's fun to play. It was a good choice for a second-half opener and we breezed through it nicely.

Then came the Rameau.

It's scored for violin, gamba, and harpsichord. Rameau himself called it a *pièce en concert*, or consort piece, but it's really a suite for harpsichord with string obbligato. The violin, which wants to take the lead, has to be throttled way back and kept quiet throughout.

This is music finer-boned, subtler, and more introverted than the music we'd been playing. It gave us some problems. I had mine with the fiddle, and Ralph had his. Boyle's harpsichord didn't have quite enough range, and we could hear Ralph swear under his breath as he reached in vain for a low A and had to settle for the one an octave higher. But none of that mattered. In seconds, we were where we'd been in the Corelli, off the face of the earth, somewhere inside our music.

And as it this weren't enough, while we were playing the moon was slowly inching up over the sea.

Huge and golden-orange when it breasted the horizon— that happened just at the end of the first movement—it changed color as it climbed the sky. By the time we finished, it was its silvery self, presiding in glory over a tropical night.

The audience responded to us. But most were as moon-struck as we were, and their clapping was subdued.

My throat was dry. I was completely used up. "We'll play you one encore," I croaked, "the Fifth Consort Piece of Rameau."

We played it.

As the last note died away, Boyle stood up. "Ladies and gentlemen," he said. "Please don't applaud. Applause would merely cheapen what we have experienced here tonight. I personally will remember this evening until the day I die."

"Oh damn," Ralph muttered, "I wish people wouldn't talk like that. It gives me the creeps."

I laughed, and I think we all did.

At that moment, exhilaration over what we'd just done was battling with sheer exhaustion. All I wanted in the world was to get offstage, unwind, and celebrate. So I laughed and patted Ralph on the shoulder and told him not to worry, Boyle would outlive us all.

But Ralph was right and I was wrong, wrong, wrong.

C H A P T E R   8

I awoke once during the night, with Jackie asleep beside me, to hear rain beating on the deck above our heads. I lay awake listening and thinking. It was fun to look back on the concert and how well we'd played. It was fun, too, though in a different way, to contemplate Jeremiah Boyle's attempt on Jackie. For several minutes, I tried to work out exactly what I felt toward Boyle. Was it amused contempt or wry amusement or wry contempt or contemptuous wryness . . . The hell with it. I went back to sleep.

"The clothespins," Jackie said suddenly at breakfast.

The rain had long since blown out to sea, the morning was clear and bright, and I'd been totally unsuccessful at persuading Jackie not to go for a prebreakfast swim. On the contrary, she'd been totally successful at luring me into the briny deep. But afterward she'd repented and towelled me dry and brought up juice and freshly baked sweet rolls and hot, hot coffee from the galley to make up for the thousands of calories I claimed to have expended in the icy waters of the Caribbean.

"Clothespins? Oh, from last night." The ones we'd used to windproof our music. "We must have left them in the salon. I'll get them later."

"Don't forget. The last time we needed clothespins, I had to go all over town before I found them."

So help me, clothespins were the only thing on my mind when I wandered into the salon in my cutoffs and sneakers and suddenly found myself smack in the middle of a heavy-weight meeting.

". . . long-tail money is great, Sir Sam, but—" The voice froze in mid sentence and seven heads swiveled in my direction.

Five of the seven were familiar. They belonged, in no particular order, to Boyle, Everett Feuerman, Atley R. Sensabaugh, the banker whose real name I kept forgetting but whose nickname was Tommy, and Hugh Jackson Shaver. Shaver was a youngish man with a short haircut, a self-contained manner, and a pretty girlfriend named Christine. They'd come on board the evening before. He and Chris were sorry, he'd told me unapologetically, but they were skipping the concert. Too much work to do.

"You must be a lawyer," I'd said to him then.

He'd nodded curtly. "I am."

The other two heads belonged to strangers. One was a distinguished type in his mid sixties wearing gold pince-nez eyeglasses. Seated close by was a younger version of the same man minus the pince-nez but sporting a neatly trimmed mustache. Father and son? Uncle and nephew?

Shaver, I saw, was giving me a what-is-this-guy-doing-here stare, as if I'd deliberately broken in on the confabulation.

"Excuse me," I said. "I came in to look for something, but I can come back later." Because of Shaver, I spoke less apologetically than I might have done otherwise.

Nobody answered.

Suits and neckties were not being worn, but there was plenty of evidence nevertheless of the kind of meeting I'd interrupted. Expensive briefcases gaped open and papers were spread all over the place. A lap-top computer was set up on a table, its screen winking solemnly at me.

I turned to go.

Finally, Boyle cleared his throat. "I'm sorry, Alan, we're being very rude. This is just a little private discussion we're having, and I guess you caught us by surprise. We won't be long, I promise. You can get in here in just a few minutes, okay?"

"Absolutely," I said. "I certainly didn't mean to interrupt."

"Of course not," Sensabaugh rumbled, but Shaver the lawyer kept on eyeballing me as if he wasn't sure. I was starting to dislike Shaver.

I left, closing the door. Of course I took nothing with me. But I have good eyes and they couldn't help seeing things.

Like the anxious look on the face of the elderly stranger.

Like the figure blinking on the computer screen: $40,000,000.

And the title on the cover of the report Boyle was holding: Strategic Plan One: For Acquisition of The Bank of Samuel Swain, Ltd., Turks & Caicos Islands.

"Don't look now," I said to Jackie a few seconds later, "but I think this yacht is a pirate ship in disguise."

"What on earth are you talking about?" she said. "And where are the clothespins?"

"The answer to your second question is, they're still in the salon. Stick around and you may get the answer to your first question."

Sure enough, the door from the salon opened and out came several of the people in the meeting. Leading the way, briefcase in hand, was Hugh Jackson Shaver.

Shaver made a beeline for us. "I'm not sure I know exactly what you meant by poking your nose into our meeting," he said. "But make sure you understand that it was a confidential business conference and that any work product you saw was private and privileged. In lay language, keep your mouth shut or face the consequences."

I resisted the temptation to poke him in the nose. But for once, words didn't fail me. "You know, I read somewhere that a really good lawyer today behaves like a hungry Doberman. You're foaming at the mouth like a Doberman, so I guess you're good, but you're snapping at the wrong party. I went into that room on business of my own. When I saw there was a meeting going on, I apologized and left. I suggest you do the same."

My combativeness didn't faze Shaver a bit. "Just remember what I said, that's all." He turned his back and walked away.

"Christus!" Jackie exclaimed. "What was that all about?"

"What I told you, the answer to your second question. When I went in to look for those damn clothespins, I interrupted a great big powwow. Look, here come two more of the sachems."

The elderly man with the gold pince-nez and his younger counterpart walked past us on their way to the companion ladder. They climbed down it one after the other and went aboard the trim motorboat made fast at the bottom. Both of them moved with the ease of men used to small boats. A man in a boatman's khaki shirt and slacks started up the outboard and the motorboat purred away from *Enchantress* and out of the cove.

"The boarders have been repelled, hurrah," I said. "Let's go get another cinnamon bun."

"You're eating too much, you're going to get terribly fat. And stop being mysterious and enigmatic."

"Isn't that why you married me?" I asked. "Because I was mysterious and enigmatic? There I sat in the dark little bar, a cigarette dangling from my lips, an enigmatic look on my mysterious face—"

"You were hoping the manager wouldn't notice that your American Express card had expired. Now for the last time, what's all this mumbo jumbo about sachems and boarders?"

"From what I saw and heard in there, our host, apart from having designs on you, is also hot for a bank. Feuerman and Sensabaugh and his other pals are in cahoots with him. I'd guess that some aspect of the deal is what those two were arguing about yesterday. I'd also be willing to bet that the two gents who just departed were the bank in question, or part of it, anyway. And they evidently have the same reaction to being taken over that I presume you have."

Jackie eyed me calmly. "You're cute when you're jealous," she said.

"Don't bet on it. Anyway, that's what I think is happening. I'm still not sure it matters very much to us, except for the deplorable effect it's having on Hugh Shaver's manners."

"But it's typical of Boyle, isn't it? A yachting party that's really a business trip, a concert that's entertainment for his guests but also, also . . ."

"An excuse to chase a new skirt. You could be right," I said, "Boyle's a bright, bright guy."

I learned another lesson in how bright within the hour.

I was prowling the boat deck in search of a quiet shady spot in which to sit with a paperback when Charlotte Sensabaugh turned a corner and headed my way. Quick as Ralph's Cat Frescobaldi, I ducked into a doorway to avoid her and found myself climbing the narrow companionway—sensible landlubbers call these things ladders—that led to the bridge.

Captain Hayward was seated at a tiny table covered with books and charts. He held a small screwdriver in one hand and a shiny piece of nautical equipment in the other. He looked up and nodded politely when he saw me, but it was plain that he was about to commit major surgery and would prefer not to be disturbed. So I turned the opposite way and went out the sliding door that led to the top deck.

Much of this was taken up by *Enchantress*'s funnel.

Much, but not all. A small area abaft the funnel was set up for sunbathing. Somebody had been using it recently, because I could still smell tanning lotion, but it was deserted now and I guessed it would be until it got cooler in midafternoon. On either side of this central space rose the characteristic curved shapes of the ventilators that brought air to the boat deck staterooms. These weren't huge affairs; they stood only a couple of feet high. But they were a perfect height for anyone who wanted to perch on a deck chair and eavesdrop on the conversation that was being piped upward from below.

This time, I felt no embarrassment or guilt, only a powerful curiosity. It was strange: as soon as I heard Boyle's voice and Feuerman's, I was absolutely determined to listen in on what they were saying. Maybe it's just a sneaky way of hitting back at Boyle, I told myself.

"Everett, it's a good approach," I heard Boyle say. "It's thoughtful and it's persuasive. Leave them in a strong minority position and guarantee them the say-so on every local loan and maybe we don't have to go another four times earnings."

"No, not *every* local loan," Feuerman was explaining, "just the important ones. Up to a big limit."

"Whatever," Boyle said. "It's still a good idea. You're saying—"

"What I'm really saying to them is that we're going to leave their little island establishment intact and undamaged. That our capital is going to help them do the things locally that they want to do for themselves. And for their friends. And not only that, but we also want to cut them in on development, international banking, reinsurance, things like that. Things of benefit to the whole economy."

"Terrific. I think it sounds terrific. Tommy, what do you think?"

"Well, it's not bad." The new voice was Williamson's.

I mopped my brow with my paperback, which was no more absorbent than most paperbacks are. The sun was broiling, but if I moved into the shade cast by the funnel, I'd have trouble hearing the quieter bits of the conversation. And I didn't want to miss a word.

"It's not bad at all," Williamson went on. "But I don't think they'll fall for it."

"What do you mean, fall for it?" Feuerman was annoyed. "This is not some kind of sales gimmick. It's a basic statement of policy."

"These people may be Brits and sirs and all that," said Williamson, "but they are also, and mostly, small-town bankers. "They've been doing the banking in these parts since . . ." I could dimly hear papers rustling. "Since eighteen thirty-one."

"So?" Feuerman again.

"Bankers know that when they're bought out, that's the end of it. Sure, you can tell that they'll still run things down here, but they'll say to themselves, sooner or later, and probably it will be sooner, we're going to want to do something New York won't want us to do. And we'll have to not do it. No. Everett, they won't buy it. What they want is money, not promises—or rather, they want money *and* promises, but if they can't get both they'll settle for money. We're already up to twelve, maybe we don't have to go all the way to sixteen times earnings, but money is what will talk, good old brownshoe money, not economic pie in the sky. Believe me, I know."

There was silence down below. I sat fascinated. This was better than *Dynasty*.

Boyle's voice was affable. "What do you say to that, Everett?"

"What do you mean, what do I say? He's wrong, that's all. The Swains may be bankers, but they're also owners. Entrepreneurs. If they wanted good old brown-shoe money"—Feuerman made it sound like leftover dogmeat—"they could sell out tomorrow. It's precisely because they want something more that they're dealing with us. And what's the more? Prestige. The idea that they, Sir Samuel Swain and Junior Swain, whatever his name is, are playing in the international big leagues. I tell you, that idea is worth a lot of money to us. Let's use it."

I heard Boyle laugh. "I doubt that Eric Swain would appreciate being called Junior."

"No, well, maybe not. But I'm right nonetheless."

"I'd hate to bet on it," Williamson shot back. "In fact, I'm not going to bet on it. Frankly, if that's going to be our pitch, then I'm afraid I won't be able to be of much help."

Feuerman didn't like that. "What are you saying? Jerry, what is Tommy saying?"

"Now calm down, both of you," Boyle said. "Calm down and listen to me. I've got some ideas on this, too. Ray, you want to hand me those notes I jotted down?"

There was a scraping of chairs and more rustling of papers. Presumably this meant they were calming down. Then Boyle spoke again. "Everett, I still think your approach is good. But Tommy has a point. I've known Sam Swain for years, and God knows he loves a lord. When he got his K, his knighthood, he threw a dinner for half the people on Grand Turk and all the people on Provo. You're right, prestige matters to him. But Sam's a lot more than your simple Sassenach snob. He's a shrewd cookie, and like a lot of these people in the Caribbean, he's been through hard times and doesn't want to go through them again.

"So the way I see it, when we make our presentation to the full board . . . Everett, you represent the best, most sophisticated multinational economic thinking. Talk to them about the opportunities that we're going to open up for them in trade financing, the Euromarket, reinsurance. Remind them of Bermuda. They're very rich in Bermuda these days.

"Tommy, you tell them the pure banking side of the story. The value of being associated with a big money-center bank and so on. And you raise the issue of autonomy in local financing: just as they can look to our expertise overseas, so we want to be able to rely on theirs at home. That's the stuff I mean."

"And what are you going to say?" Williamson asked.

Boyle laughed. "Oh, I think I'll just mix them a little snake oil and strychnine cocktail."

Laughter.

"The snake oil will be the powerful economic and banking expertise you gentlemen represent. Plus of course our hands-off policy as regards their, shall we say, more favored local customers."

"And the strychnine?" I wasn't surprised that it was Feuerman who asked. I figured he'd take an interest in poisons.

"The strychnine is those nasty rumors being put about by the competition. That The Bank of Samuel Swain Limited has bought itself a couple of drums of detergent and is now running a money Laundromat on behalf of certain clients who are, um, entrepreneurs of substance. Of substances, rather. Controlled ones. Rumors like that don't exactly add lustre to a bank's reputation."

"Not in the mind of the comptroller of the U.S. currency," Williamson said.

"Exactly," Boyle said.

"Or the Drug Enforcement Administration," Feuerman added.

"Those lads likewise," said Boyle. "I think I'd go on to say that alliance with people like us, quite apart from all the other benefits appurtenant thereunto, would instantly squelch those rumors."

"It's a good point, Jerry," Feuerman said, "but it's a good point on the negative side."

"Yeah," said Williamson, "we don't want to be *too* negative."

"Of course not," Boyle said smoothly. "That's why I want you two to go first. Then I can just delicately hint around the subject. I know the one or two people on the board who are really nervous about these malicious and, need I say, unfounded allegations."

One thing about Feuerman, he didn't give up easily.

"Well, I still think we'd be better off tying local autonomy to a slightly lower offer. I'd like to open at fourteen."

"And I still think these guys are going to laugh at anything short of sixteen," Williamson retorted. "That's our forty million, and I think we ought to shell it out and get it over with."

Holy cow.

"It's good to take the time to talk these things over," Boyle said pleasantly. "But right now time is running out. Is it agreed that Tommy's going to talk banking and autonomy and Everett, you're going to spread out the multinational caviar?"

Silence.

Suddenly, Boyle's voice turned cold. "Well, is it or isn't it? If it is, I want to hear you say so. And let's keep one thing in mind. I can get Shaver up here in one second and turn this deal *off*. Everett, you wouldn't like that, would you? It's not cheap, operating without the State Department to pick up your tab, and I know you, you love to paint with a real broad brush. And Tommy, with what's been happening to First Trust's own earnings the past five years, I'll bet you wouldn't like it either, not one damn bit. So let's end the argument and settle this, and I mean now."

More silence, which Feuerman was the first to break. "I'll do it," he snapped. "If Tommy agrees." A second later, I heard Williamson grunt his acquiescence. But I wouldn't have wanted to lead a patrol out in front of either of them.

Boyle said something else, but I never did find out what: when I leaned forward to listen more closely I banged the metal frame of the deck chair against the ventilator.

There was an immediate hush down below.

"Ray, check that out for us, will you?" Boyle said quietly, and I knew I was in trouble.

I could try to make it down the companionway. But the chances were one hundred percent that Gerard and his .357 Magnum would be coming *up* while I was coming *down*.

Alternatively, I could stretch out in my chair and pretend to be fast asleep. But the temperature on the top deck, even in the shadow of the funnel, must have been well over 120 degrees, and nobody in his right mind, as Gerard would well know, lies down for a nice little snooze in a frying pan.

Gerard wasn't going to shoot me, was he? He liked me. All the same, I really didn't relish the idea of his finding me here. Things other than shooting might ensue. Bad, unpleasant things. And in a few seconds, he was going to find me. I could hear his deliberate footsteps on the companionway. I could hear him whistling tunelessly between his teeth.

Instinctively, not knowing what else to do, I moved to put the bulk of the funnel between myself and the doorway through which Gerard would shortly be coming.

That's when I spotted the ladder.

It wasn't a real ladder with treads and side rails, just a set of rungs leading up the side of the funnel all the way to the top. And it wasn't much of a place of refuge, but it was the only one I had.

Musicians think of their hands always. Before I reached for the first rung and started climbing, I peeled off my shirt and wrapped a couple of layers of the material around my fingers. It was lucky I did. Even through the shirting, the metalwork was hot enough to be painful. Using my hands with the shirt stretched between them was awkward, but I managed. The top of the funnel was about fifteen feet above the deck, and I reached it and hiked myself up and perched on the foot-wide lip, feeling horribly exposed and conspicuous. I froze—a ludicrous word for it in that heat—when the sound of footsteps and that chirpy whistling told me that Gerard was below me, hidden by the swell of the funnel but clearly present and looking around.

In the quiet, I could hear a scrape of metal. Gerard was moving the deck chair, probably pulling it clear of the ventilator. Maybe he'd think a sudden puff of wind had blown it over, even though the morning had been and still was absolutely windless. Maybe he'd think a rhinoceros had lumbered out of the bridge house, toppled the deck chair, and lumbered back inside.

I could feel my shoulders frying in the sun. A few minutes more and I'd be toppling over myself, from heat-stroke. Why the hell didn't Gerard *finish*?

In reality, it couldn't have been more than twenty seconds before he did finish. I could still hear him moving around, but the whistling grew fainter. Was he please God leaving? He must be, I thought, and I was right. By craning my neck I could just see his shoulders and the top of his head disappear through the door that led to the bridge.

Slowly and carefully, wincing at every tiny noise I made, I climbed down.

Voices were once again coming from the ventilator but I ignored them. My paroxysm of curiosity was more than satisfied. Wondering why I'd been so curious in the first place, I put my shirt back on and got the hell out of there.

CHAPTER 9

he shower in our cabin may have been cramped, but it did the job. I stood under it for about ten minutes with the spray turned to lukewarm and began to feel a little less like a wilted lettuce leaf.

As I was toweling myself dry, Jackie came in. "Where have you been? You've gotten very red."

I explained. It went better than I hoped. When I got to the part about Boyle's planning a little genteel blackmail on the issue of laundering money for drug dealers, Jackie stopped being angry with me for being a busybody and started being angry at Boyle. When I told her about shinnying up the funnel to hide from Gerard, she smiled but her eyes were worried. "Do you think they know it was you out there?"

"No. How could they?"

"I don't know," she said, "but I don't like it. It sounds as if what they're doing isn't just dirty; it sounds as if it could be dangerous."

Considering what Gerard packed under his coat, I had to wonder if she wasn't right. Nor would Boyle be the only one to be upset. Feuerman and Williamson would be even madder. "Those guys have egos almost as big as Boyle's, but Boyle treated them like third-graders. He laughed at them for being money hungry. He threatened to kill the deal altogether if they didn't get in line and play things his way. They got in line, but they weren't happy. If they knew I'd heard all that, they'd go ballistic. God knows what they'd do."

"I hope Boyle's dirty deal falls through," Jackie said. "I hope he loses all forty million dollars and more besides. I hope he goes bankrupt like my cousin Dilbert."

"Cut it out," I said. "I met all your cousins at our wedding and you don't have any Cousin Dilbert."

"I do too. He's Uncle Colvin's eldest. You remember Uncle Colvin, don't you?"

"Sure. He's the one who wouldn't let you practice because it kept the cows awake. Nice guy."

"Dilbert's just like his father, only worse," Jackie said. "He didn't come to the wedding."

"Why was that?" I asked. "Because he's bankrupt?"

"Oh, he's not bankrupt anymore. He got out of that years ago. Daddy and one of my other uncles lent him the money. Now he's selling Toyotas over in Veedersburg and doing very well."

"In where?" Jackie's relatives are scattered all across western Indiana.

"Veedersburg. South of us, right near the state line."

"Oh," I said, not much wiser and not wanting to be. "Well, good for Dilbert. I'm glad."

"Don't be. He's hateful. You have to watch him all the time or he'll do something mean and nasty to you. Now get dressed. It's nearly lunchtime and I'm starving."

On the way out the door, I paused. "Do you really think Boyle and his buddies are dangerous?"

Jackie made a face. "I don't know about the buddies," she said, "but I've had Boyle's hands on me and, yes, I think he could be. I was just something he fancied for the moment. But if it was something he really wanted, yes. He'd do anything to get it. Underneath those nice Wasp manners, don't forget, he's crazy Irish."

By the time we arrived on the boat deck a crew member was tapping the gong for lunch. David, Ralph, and Terry were waiting for us, and we all filed into the dining room together.

The women, even Jackie, were saying "Oooh" and "Look how beautiful," and I didn't blame them. Boyle or Hayward or somebody had sent ashore for fresh flowers for the tables, and the china and glassware and silver sparkled against the starched off-white linen. The effect was studiedly, crisply informal, like the dining room of a very expensive New York restaurant that wanted to be taken for the dining room of a very expensive New York home.

Boyle, Feuerman, and Williamson came in as the rest of us were taking our seats. I watched them settle in. None of them showed the least sign of having been in an argument. On the contrary, they were as relaxed, as unruffled as if they'd just finished a friendly round of golf. Feuerman's face was a shade less pasty than usual, I thought, but that could easily have been sunburn. Amazing. We spend our lives learning how to express ourselves in music; these guys learn in the cradle how to put on masks and cover themselves up.

The two stewards in their white mess jackets took away our soup cups. They'd just begun serving the main course—I seem to remember a curried seafood salad—when Kitty Feuerman blew the tranquil atmosphere to smithereens.

She and Boyle were sitting across from one another at the next table. If there hadn't been one of those accidental lulls that sometimes overtake a roomful of talk, we might never have heard her opening salvo, and maybe things aboard *Enchantress* would have turned out differently. But there was a lull, and in the middle of it Kitty's voice, though not especially loud, came through like a bouzouki clarinet.

"Why, Jerry! You remember perfectly well. That speech was a disaster. You were *awful*."

Everybody turned to look. Kitty was smiling. When I saw that smile, I wanted to leave the room.

"He was awful, everybody, can you imagine? Jeremiah Boyle, our boy wonder, Hotchkiss, Yale, London School of Economics, the most perceptive political mind of his generation, telling a bunch of New York City CPAs about Edmund Burke! *They* wanted to know how soon his bosom buddy the president was going to cut taxes and *he* was telling them to study the French Revolution. What a fiasco!"

She stopped for breath—she had to—and Boyle cut in immediately. He did it nicely, I must say. "Kitty's dead right," he declared with what sounded like genuine good humor. "It was the most dreadful speech I ever made. Every time I think about it I go goosebumps with embarrassment. Those poor accountants! And poor Kitty! You were upset, weren't you?"

For a minute, it seemed as if Boyle's gallant display had saved the day. I remember spearing a chunk of lobster on my fork but not having time to dip it in the sauce before Kitty started up again.

"But that wasn't the worst," she cried. "The worst was what happened after the dinner. The head of the CPAs came up to Jerry and congratulated him on his speech, which was such a nice thing to do, and you know what Jerry said? He said, and frankly he was looking down his nose, weren't you Jerry? He said, 'I'm really sorry, I thought I was talking to the Center for Political Analysis.' C-P-A, get it? 'If I had known, I would have given a much *simpler* speech.' The poor head CPA just turned beet red and walked away. Well, heavens, what would you have done?"

God knows what she would have said next, but once again she paused for breath and once again Boyle interrupted. I wondered what on earth he'd find to say this time, and I wasn't alone. The room went rigid with shock and embarrassment. Simultaneously, of course, we were all drooling to hear more.

"Kitty. How many times have I told you." Boyle's voice was soft, almost caressing. "It's not *nice* to tell tales like that. People might get the wrong idea, mightn't they?"

She waited a long time to answer. I had the feeling that she was beginning to regret the impulse that made her launch her attack. "They might," she said. "But then again they might get the *right* idea."

It was Boyle's turn to stretch his lips in a kind of smile. "True, very true. But Kitty, they'd get the right idea about *you*, not me. They'd imagine that anyone who would tell a story like that in public has to be . . . ill-educated. Perhaps even crude."

"Jerry, hush! You mustn't say such things." Probably only Sally Boyle in the whole world would have dared to break in at this point, but she didn't hesitate for a second. "And Kitty dear, you, too. This really is a bit *untraveled* of you."

Sally's mild adjective, so carefully chosen, so dispassionately spoken, made Kitty go white and silent in her chair.

Somebody laughed nervously.

"All right, Mother, I apologize," said Boyle, "I shouldn't have said what I said. Fair enough. But I mean, for God's sake! Tell me, Kitty, do you even know who Edmund Burke *was*? No? I thought not. They didn't teach much history at—where was it you went, Bennington?—did they.

"No, don't interrupt," Boyle said, "we're talking about you now, not me. We've agreed you don't have much of a historical sense, but what about belles lettres? You've read Montaigne, haven't you? Spinoza? Bacon's *Essays*? Bolingbroke? Well, surely you've read Addison on the uses of politeness, and Chesterfield's letters, and Walpole's. Oh. You don't have the time. But you do have the time to go on yacht trips with me and spew out your gossip to my friends, my guests."

"For Christ's sake, Jerry . . ." It was Shaver who spoke.

Boyle didn't even bother to ignore him. "Well. If you can't be troubled with what serious people say on the subject of behavior, you ought to try Emily Post or Amy Vanderbilt. I'm sure you'd be able to understand *them*. Now, say you're sorry so we can eat our lunch."

I'll never forget the look on Kitty's face. It was the look of someone dead in a wayside ambush. Without a word, without even a dry sob, she rose from the table and left the room.

I stole a glance at Everett Feuerman. He made no effort to follow his wife. On the contrary, he just sat there like the rest of us, his face bloodless, staring at his folded hands.

"I apologize profoundly," Boyle said to the room. "It was a shocking thing for Kitty to do. Please don't let it spoil your meal." But of course it already had. Conversation stopped dead. Even David stopped eating after the obligatory three forkfuls.

Everybody was relieved when Boyle himself dropped his napkin on the table, said a few words to the people near him, and got to his feet. Within seconds, we had all followed suit.

We could overhear Boyle explaining in the passageway outside. "Hugh, what can I say? She gets this way at times and there's nothing else to do."

Nothing except flay her in public? Shaver, certainly no shrinking violet when it came to verbal abuse, grunted noncommittally. Ralph's eyebrows went up and Jackie was pushing icily past when Boyle held out an arm to bar our way. "Please. Wait one minute. I need you for something."

I kept an anxious eye on Jackie, but though her face reddened dangerously under her tan she kept her mouth firmly shut. I touched her hand gratefully. Terry shrugged and David made a what-the-hell face, but I knew we were all curious, even Jackie, so we let Boyle shepherd us into the salon.

"First things first," he said crisply. "I'm awfully sorry you had to sit through all that. Kitty—Mrs. Feuerman—is such a nice person, but she is a little high-strung, and at times I'm afraid she goes just a wee bit off the rails."

At first the man's effrontery stunned me, but then I

realized that it shouldn't. Boyle had no idea that we'd been listening to below-stairs, or rather, above-stairs gossip. That we'd been told he and Kitty were lovers. He was just advancing what he thought would be a plausible explanation for an embarrassing episode.

Jackie couldn't hold back any longer. "What about you? Weren't you just a wee bit off the rails yourself?"

Boyle looked dismayed. "My dear girl," he began.

"I'm not a girl and I'm not your dear anything," Jackie said.

Boyle looked even more dismayed. Then the corners of his eyes crinkled. "Oh, indeed," he said, "you're not, of course. But surely you won't begrudge an old dog like me his old tricks. What I meant to say was, yes, I suppose I did get a little upset, but can you blame me? I did try to be pleasant at first, after all. You remember the French poet, don't you? The one who said *'Quel animal méchant! Quand on l'attaque, il se défend.'* All I did was defend myself.

"Anyway, that's not what I brought you here for. What I really have in mind is something more up your alley. Professionally, that is."

Oh oh.

Boyle was already moving toward the harpsichord. "Of course you know I play." He laughed a little self-consciously. "As a favor, would you listen to something I've been working on and just tell me whether I'm doing it properly? You especially, Ralph, but you others, too. Now, don't hesitate to say exactly what you think, even if you think I'm terrible. Okay then . . . here goes."

Before any of us could stop him, he launched into the majestic opening of Rameau's wonderful A minor Gavotte et Doubles.

We stood there embarrassedly and listened: what else could we do?

Boyle was less awful than many of the enthusiastic amateurs I've had to listen to over the years. He'd obviously been well taught, and he'd learned the music by heart. The first three *doubles* or variations went smoothly, and he stayed nearly up to tempo in the more complicated third. He only broke down once, in the very difficult fourth variation, and then he didn't make any excuses or mutter curses to himself, he simply stopped, took a deep breath and started again.

If your standard of musical performance is getting the notes right, Boyle didn't do too badly. But getting the notes right, of course, is only part of it. And it was all too clear to me what was missing and why.

Part of Boyle's problem was strength. His fingers, unconditioned by the pro's hours of daily playing and years of practice, weren't up to anything this long and demanding. Being Boyle, he didn't understand this, he thought he was in control, but long before he broke down, muscle fatigue was making his touch heavy on the keys.

But the heart of the problem wasn't mechanics, it was . . . soul. The same cockiness that made Boyle tackle the Rameau in the first place virtually guaranteed that he wouldn't give much thought to its meaning. Here was Rameau, like a man blowing up a beautiful red balloon a puff at a time, putting forth one variation after another to expand a simple theme into something huge and majestic, and all Boyle could see in this was a showpiece for Boyle.

At last it was over. Boyle sat for a second as if drinking in the final arpeggio, then turned to us, his forehead damp, with the dreaded question: "How was it?"

For a second, nobody spoke at all.

Jackie bit her lip. Terry shoved his hands deep in the pockets of his brick-colored slacks. David gazed raptly out the window.

Ralph looked at me for a cue, but I carefully avoided his eye. What the hell, he was the harpsichordist. He was also, as well I knew, quite able to handle situations like this one. More than that, he enjoyed them. "Nice," he said to Boyle, perhaps a shade too politely. "Parts of it were lovely."

"No, really, for God's sake," Boyle protested, "what did you think?"

Ralph regarded Boyle judiciously. "Well. You were start-ing cold. I always feel the Rameau is hard to get into without a warm-up."

"Yes, absolutely. I should have thought of that."

"And then . . . probably you aren't quite used to this instrument."

"No, that's right," said Boyle. "It sounds much better on my two-manual Shudi back in New York. *Much* smoother."

"And I'll bet you haven't had much time to practice lately."

"No," Boyle confessed. "Things just keep getting in the way."

Having anesthetized his victim, Ralph picked up his scalpel. "If I were you," he said, "I think I'd start working on some, um, less *complicated* pieces. Maybe a little Purcell, some of the shorter Rameau. Go slowly. And practice each hand separately. That would help you loosen up a little bit."

"Oh." Boyle's face fell. They never like to be told they're tackling material that's nine times too hard for them.

"And don't forget your good old Czerny," Ralph said blithely, referring to the book of stupefyingly boring exercises every keyboard student knows and loathes.

"I'll try not to," Boyle said. He didn't sound happy, and no wonder. In a few bland comments, Ralph had reduced him from polished amateur to floundering beginner, and the worst thing about it was that he'd asked for it, in fact begged for it.

"Trust me," Ralph went on with ruthless cordiality. "Keep on playing and you'll do beautiful work."

"Okay," Boyle said. "Now you, Jackie. What did you think?" A teasing note crept into his voice. "Surely you're not going to be as hard on me as Ralph is?"

"Harder," Jackie said succinctly.

"What do you mean, harder?"

She thought for a moment. "I guess I mean that you try to bully the harpsichord the same way you bully people.

Maybe it works with people, some people anyway, but it doesn't with the harpsichord."

Boyle went a touch white around the mouth. "I've never thought of myself as a bully," he said stiffly.

Jackie smiled at him. "You're not one all the time," she said. "Just sometimes. But when you're being one, it shows up in your playing. I'm sorry. I wish I could say something nicer. Maybe if you didn't play when you were tired or upset . . ."

If it had been me, I would have prayed for *Enchantress* to split in two and for the Caribbean to swallow me alive. But not Boyle. Boyle was made of sterner stuff. An aggrieved smile replaced the momentary shock on his face. "I must admit I was a bit off form just now," he said, "but really, Jackie, to make a personal judgment like that on the basis of one run-through of one piece . . . Surely you'll want to reconsider. When you do, of course, I'll be delighted to listen."

My God, I thought, he believes every word. In his own mind, he's still a terrific harpsichordist. And an irresistible lover as well.

Jackie started to say something, caught sight of the look on my face, and gave up.

Hypnotized, we watched Boyle play out the scene.

He slapped a hand on the lid of the harpsichord to remind it that, no matter what Jackie said, he was its master. Then he stood up. "I'd love to stay," he said. "In fact, I'd love to be able to give my whole life to music, the way you people do. But we can't always do the things we'd like, can we? Anyway, thank you all very much. Afraid I'm going to be pretty tied up the next two days, but let's hope we can spend some more time together before we ship you home. Meanwhile, do enjoy the rest of your stay on board."

In control again, his self-esteem miraculously undented, Boyle smiled the quick, practiced smile that was meant to charm the hoi polloi and sometimes did, and marched out the door as if he'd just won a medal from the Bach Society.

CHAPTER 10

*S*till not quite believing what we'd just heard, we wandered up the companionway and out onto the boat deck. We were the only ones there. Boyle must have stayed below with his male buddies. The women too were nowhere to be seen, though some, Sally Boyle among them, had decided that the thing to do was play bridge. We could hear them doing it through a cabin porthole. The sky was still cloudless and the air still balmy, but the relaxed, mellow, all-friends-together atmosphere of yesterday was gone. In its place was emptiness.

We did our best to ignore it. The deck steward, a nice guy if ever there was one, brought us ice and drinks and bowls of goodies to eat, just as if we were proper guests and not, as he was, people paid to be there. We sat by the rail, sipping lime Perrier and Diet Coke and in David's case real Coke, and watched seabirds work the cove for dinner. And we talked, mostly about Jeremiah Boyle and his little ways.

"I can't understand the guy," Terry said for the fourth time.

I just shook my head.

"Simple," said David, "he's one of those people, he closes his eyes and all over the world it's night."

"You're right, it *is* simple," said Ralph. "He's rich, cultivated, gentlemanly, and a monster."

"I don't think he's a monster exactly," Jackie corrected, "but he's well on his way."

"Lunch," Ralph said, "an unforgettable experience. Can you imagine what dinner will be like?"

"Please let's not worry about it," Jackie said. "Let's just enjoy ourselves. One more day and we fly back to New York."

The afternoon drifted on. It grew hotter and hotter, and finally we all changed into suits and went for a swim, but swimming didn't help much. The memory of the day's events was too strong. When we came out, we were still fidgety and ill at ease.

We were mopping ourselves dry on deck when a sudden loud crack from the direction of the stern went reverberating around the cove. It was followed by shouts. We all jumped.

"Jesus," Terry breathed. "It happened. Somebody took the guy down."

We rushed to the stern and looked over the rail at the tableau on the fantail.

Terry was wrong: Boyle was very much alive. He, Feuerman, Williamson, Shaver, Sensabaugh—all the men were there, grouped by the rail. They seemed to be looking out to sea. Boyle had a big pair of binoculars slung around his neck. Hayward in his khakis and white captain's hat was there too. He was holding a gun, a heavy rifle. As we watched, he proffered it to Sensabaugh, but Sensabaugh stepped back and smilingly shook his head. A couple of the others did likewise.

Not Feuerman.

He looked awkward and rumpled as usual in his light blue shorts. I could see the matted gray chest hair sticking out of the collar of his matching blue Lacoste shirt. But there was nothing awkward about the way he took the rifle when Hayward passed it over. He handled it knowingly, much the way I'd handle an unfamiliar violin, getting the feel of it, assessing its balance and weight. Then with a smooth expert movement he brought the stock to his shoulder, took aim, and fired. As far as I could tell, he was shooting into the water by the entrance to the cove.

For a long moment, nothing happened. Boyle lowered his binoculars and started to turn to Feuerman, shaking his head, when Hayward yelled and pointed.

Even without binoculars, I could see the water at the entrance suddenly grow foamy and agitated, as though somebody was stirring it with a giant spoon. Then from the midst of the foam a fish so huge that it took my breath away arched into the air and hung there motionless, poised for so long that I thought I could see the droplets of water fly sparkling from its sides as it shook itself in mid flight. At the high point of that leap, the fish must have been twenty feet up. Then it dropped straight down, hitting the surface with a smack even louder than the gunshot, sending the seabirds, already scared by the shooting, into even more frantic spiralings.

I sucked in my breath in awe. But during that downward plunge I saw the ugly reality behind the spectacular performance. The water cascading off the fish's back was running deep red.

"Oh Christ. Jackie, don't look," Terry said beside me.

Feuerman hadn't missed after all.

A chorus of approval sounded as the others crowded around him, slapping him on the back, applauding his marksmanship. I noticed that he took pains to keep the rifle pointed down and well away from his admirers. Careful man, Feuerman.

The fish jumped again, feebly, this time barely lifting its

body above the surface before falling back. Its strength was gone. I didn't think there'd be a third jump.

There was more shouting.

Jackie made a noise in her throat and turned her head away.

Boyle waved up at us. "What about that? Fantastic shot, wasn't it?"

"Yeah, great," I said.

Even Boyle couldn't miss my lack of enthusiasm, or the fact that the rest of us weren't exactly jumping up and down. "What the hell," he called up to us, "it was only a shark."

As he said it, I saw his face change. I glanced around. Kitty Feuerman had come out on deck. She was still in the dress she had worn at lunchtime. Her eyes were glassy. She focused them on me but I wasn't the one she wanted to talk to. "Are they at it again?"

"At what again?" I said.

"You know, their Hemingway thing. They do it every trip. Take turns shooting at a big fish until somebody hits it, usually Everett. Everett's a great shot with a rifle, you know. Then they watch the fish jump until it dies. They like that. You like that, don't you, Everett?" she called loudly to her husband. "Don't you?"

"Killing sharks I do," he said. "Why not? They're horrible."

"Oh. Sharks." Kitty laughed. "Sharks."

"What's wrong?" I said.

"That was no shark, the fish you just shot," she said to Feuerman. "You sportsman. It was a marlin."

Feuerman didn't answer.

"It was a shark, Kitty," Boyle said.

Kitty didn't answer, either. For a moment, the three of them stood staring at one another. Then Everett Feuerman, still holding the rifle, still keeping it pointed at the deck, worked the bolt to open the chamber and handed it to Hayward. "Fine weapon," he said. "You take excellent care of it."

"I do my best," said Hayward.

"Good man," Feuerman said. "Now for Christ's sake let's all go have a drink."

They started to drift into the salon.

"They're gun freaks, you know," Kitty said to the air. "He even keeps a gun in his bedside table. Deadeye Jerry. He showed it to me once." She made a pistol of her thumb and index finger and pointed it more or less in Boyle's direction. She raised her voice slightly. "I can shoot, too, see? Bang! You're dead!"

Boyle didn't hear, or if he did he gave no sign. Kitty's hand dropped to her side. "That gun. I made him promise never to take it out in my presence again," she said. "Now if you'll excuse me, I think I'll go back to my cabin."

"Are you okay? Can I get you anything?" Jackie asked automatically.

Kitty must have been drinking vodka, because you couldn't smell alcohol on her, but only sheer willpower was keeping her upright. She peered at Jackie. "You really are very sweet, dear," she said with surprise in her voice. She enunciated every word flawlessly, as if she was taking an elocution test. "Very sweet. But no, I'll just go and lie down for a while. And then. I'll be. Perfectly. All. Right."

Lie down? It looked to me as if Kitty was about to collapse at our feet. But before it could happen, a door banged open and Charlotte Sensabaugh came out on deck. What she saw didn't seem to surprise her. "C'mon, Kits," she said briskly, "off we go. What you need is the usual, a couple of aspirin and a cool washcloth on the forehead."

Without a word, Kitty let Charlotte lead her away.

Charlotte reappeared alone ten minutes later. "I got some aspirin in her and put her to bed," she reported. "She'll doze off now, I hope. In a couple of hours, she should feel a lot better."

"You deserve a medal, you really do," I said, "for service above and beyond the call of duty to an old college roommate."

"I second that," said Ralph.

She chuckled. "Right now I'd settle for a drink of my own. A *very* light gin and tonic."

"Let me get it for you," Jackie said. She went off to find the steward.

"You have to understand. When Kitty's herself, she's really darling," said Charlotte. "She was wonderful to me at Smith. You know, a classic case of the ugly duckling befriended by the swan."

"I don't see Kitty as an ugly duckling," I said.

"Stop being silly. I was the ugly duckling and you know it. Still am, as far as that goes," she added matter-of-factly. "It was Kitty who gave me the confidence to not worry about it and just be myself. I owe her a lot. I'd do just about anything for her." She laughed a little awkwardly. "I guess I have, from time to time."

Jackie came back and handed her her drink. "I think she's lucky to have you for a friend."

"Thank you. I can call you Jackie, can't I? Thank you, Jackie. You know, I want to tell you something." She took a long sip and regarded Jackie seriously over the rim of her glass. "Kitty thinks you're a nice person. She wants me to tell you that. Nice and very gifted. She knows it's not your fault that Jerry is, well, *interested* in you."

"Hmph," I said. "If Miss Kitty thinks that, why doesn't she say so herself?"

Charlotte froze me with one of those looks women reserve for ignorant, interfering males.

"Oh, honestly," Jackie said, "this is so embarrassing. I don't think Jeremiah Boyle is that interested in me at all. And I'm certainly not interested in *him*. Anyway, tomorrow's the last day. We'll all be leaving and going back to New York and that will be the end of it."

Charlotte looked amused. "Jackie, darling, if you think Jerry Boyle is going to stop chasing you just because you're back in New York, you don't know Jerry Boyle."

"Don't you think I'll have something to say about that?" I said.

"Of course you will. Eventually. Eventually, Jerry will realize that he's making a damn fool of himself and that the two of you are laughing at him. Then he'll stop. But I want to warn you. It could take weeks."

Jackie and I exchanged horrified glances. It hadn't occurred to me and I know it hadn't crossed her mind that that we might have to cope with Boyle, love-struck or not, beyond tomorrow.

"Hey Jackie," David said. "Now you know what I go through."

Jackie stared at him. Slowly, deadpan, she narrowed her eyes and wiggled her fingers in the sign of the *strega*, the witchcraft sign Terry had showed her a year ago.

Terry laughed.

"Okay, okay," David said, "I'm sorry. I apologize."

Suddenly we were all laughing, Charlotte too. "Maybe you should try *that* on Jerry," she said. "Maybe *that* would calm him down."

"Is he always like this?" I asked her.

"Oh, no. Basically it's nerves. It's these macho boat trips, and there's this takeover the boys are working on, and of course he's got a new girl. I don't mean you, darling," she said to Jackie, "I mean Lauren Winship. Having a new girl always gets him going."

"But . . . I mean, Kitty . . ."

Charlotte sighed. "Kitty and Jerry have been lovers for eight—no, it's nine years, ever since they met at a political fund-raiser in Washington. She's lived through five or six of his girls since, and she'll survive this one too. Speaking of which, I think I'll just take a quick look to see if the patient is okay. If you'll all forgive me." Charlotte set down her empty glass and got to her feet. Fanning herself with her straw hat, she set off in the direction of Kitty's cabin.

"You know," David said, "except for us she may be the only human being aboard this tub."

"I wouldn't want to argue with you," Ralph said. "People who like taking potshots at fish, ugh! I'm going down to get cool, shower, dress, and write some postcards. I'll see you all at dinner."

"Good idea," said Terry, "I think we'll do the same."

The three of them took off.

"You, too?" I asked.

"Let's go," Jackie said.

Later, damp from her shower, she curled up in my arms on the bed. She was wearing nothing but a smile and her wedding ring. I stroked her silky hair. "It's not so good, is it, catching a hotshot's fancy?"

"It's gross. I came down here to play music, not fend off hands."

"You're not fending off mine."

I felt her smile against my cheek. "No, never yours. Alan?"

"Mmm?"

"Are you jealous?"

"No. Yes. Passionately. Murderously. And not just of Boyle, of everybody. Grrr." I nibbled her ear. "What time is it?"

She lay quiet for a few seconds. Then she said in dignified tones, "If by that you mean, is there enough time to do what you're thinking of doing before that damn gong rings for dinner, the answer is yes."

As usual, Jackie was right. When the gong did ring, we were up, dressed, and remarkably hungry.

Dinner, when the time came for it, proved relaxed, civilized, and mercifully uneventful. Neither Kitty nor Boyle made an appearance and Shaver, too, was absent. Everett Feuerman, neatly dressed, hair slicked down, took the sixth place at our table and chatted entertainingly about life in the State Department. It sounded surprisingly like life in a big-city symphony orchestra.

Charlotte Sensabaugh, reassured after one sharp glance in our direction, sat with Captain Hayward and her husband.

The only mildly untoward event occurred just before dessert.

One of the stewards came in from outside and handed Feuerman a note.

He glanced at it, then rose and excused himself. "My master's voice. I hope I won't be too long," he said. He wasn't. The ice cream in his coupe aux framboises hadn't had time to melt before he was back in his seat. He dug into it greedily and when it was done he ordered a second bowlful. "It's a vice of mine, ice cream," he explained as he spooned it in.

Considering what Feuerman, Kitty Feuerman, Boyle, and most of the others had done with their day, an ice cream habit seemed laughably innocent. I remember thinking that he must have heard some good news to give him such a hearty appetite. But for some reason Feuerman's little confession made me curious about something else.

"Where did you learn to shoot like that?" I asked him.

"Army," he grunted, wiping his mouth, throwing down his napkin and getting up to leave.

Out on deck, another semitropical sunset spectacular was unfolding. The tireless stewards were serving coffee and liqueurs. Jackie and I took ours to a small table and sat together to enjoy the evening. But within thirty seconds I was jumping to my feet to fetch another chair. Sally Boyle had elected to join us.

"Dear Jackie, dear Alan. You really must think we are the most tiresome people. That scene at lunch! And it's taken me all this time to corner you to thank you for the beautiful concert last night. But please say you forgive us."

I mumbled words to the effect that there was nothing to forgive.

"You are sweet to say so." But Sally had more than a polite apology on her agenda. "You know, one hears so much of the artistic temperament. But most of the artists I've met, like the two of you, are of singularly even disposition. It's the nonartistic intellectual, and I'm afraid I must include poor Jerry in that category, who seems more given to displays of temperament."

Not to mention vanity, arrogance, and denial of reality.

Of course, I didn't say that. All I said was, "You ask Jackie if I have an even disposition."

"Does he, my dear?"

"Basically he does," said my treasonable better half, "but he'd rather die than admit it."

"I'll get you for that, you see if I don't," I growled.

We all laughed, and Sally Boyle led us on one of her delightful forays into the past. She brought to life grim old Boyle uncles who terrorized their nieces and nephews. We heard about Boyle's grandfather, who was so evil-natured that only bribes would entice his grandchildren to his birthday parties. Another Boyle had been excommunicated for threatening to dump his parish priest into a horse trough, or it might have been a dung heap. They were wonderful yarns, but why was she spinning them to us? Was it just for fun, or was she trying to excuse Jeremiah Boyle for being, as she put it, "difficult"? I couldn't decide.

Difficult. A word that in a mother's eyes could cover every sin in the book.

"I'll tell you one thing," I said when Sally had finished.

"And what is that?"

I smiled when I said it, but I meant it. "Jeremiah Boyle doesn't deserve you."

"Why, that's exactly what he says himself!"

I couldn't think of a comeback to that.

All of a sudden, I found myself stifling a huge yawn and watching Jackie do exactly the same thing. The long, long day had finally caught up with us. We made our excuses to Sally, who was all sympathy, and headed below to bed.

"He doesn't, either," I remarked to Jackie a few minutes later.

"Who doesn't what?"

"Boyle doesn't deserve a mother like Sally."

"It's all very well, your being madly in love with her," Jackie said, kicking off her shoes.

"I wouldn't miss it for anything," I said. "I'm probably the ten thousandth man that woman has enslaved."

"Well, don't let your heart run away with your head."

"What are you trying to tell me?"

"Maybe her dear Jerry doesn't deserve her. If you ask me, he's a bigger rat even than his grandpa, and Sally Boyle probably knows it. But Sally Boyle is a Boyle. First, last, and always."

CHAPTER   11

In the stillness, I sensed rather than heard Jackie slip out of bed. "What's wrong?" I whispered.

"Nothing. But I'm not sleeping. I'm going to go up on deck to have a look at the stars."

"Well, put something on. And watch out for Boyle."

"Of course, silly."

The cabin door shut quietly behind her. I lay half awake, waiting for her to finish her astronomy lesson and come back to bed. It didn't take as long as I thought it might.

"Br-r-r. It was cold out there."

"I know," I said, "your feet are freezing. What did you expect? It's one o'clock in the morning."

"Yes, but it was beautiful. So clear. I saw Cepheus and Cassiopeia and Arcturus . . . You're not even listening."

"Yes I am. You saw Cassius . . . Cephiopeia . . . Beware of Cassius, he hath a lean and hungry look, such men are dangerous."

We laughed together in the dark and then we went right to sleep.

I was drifting slowly and beautifully through the dark blue waters of the cove. It was wonderful. In a moment I would surface—not to breathe, I had no need for that—but to leap high, high into the sunlit air. There would be a shot, then another and another, but they would miss. . . .

Suddenly I was wide awake and listening.

I heard a scuffling of feet outside in the passageway, a brief, muffled exclamation, and a soft but insistent banging on our door. "Please, please, come quick!"

Jackie sat up beside me. "Who's that? Who is it?"

"It's me, Charlotte. Please, you've got to come! Something's happened to Jerry!"

"We're coming," I said. We threw on clothes and opened the door. Charlotte Sensabaugh, in a bathrobe, hurried ahead of us down the passage toward the salon.

"In here."

We pushed through the swinging doors and stopped short.

All the lights were on. Boyle, his back to us, sat slumped over the keyboard of the harpsichord. His left arm rested on the lid as if for balance. His right hung straight down, the fingers a few inches from the floor. His forehead was propped against the edge of the music desk. I noticed for the first time the beginning of a bald spot on his crown, with the hair combed carefully over it. I don't know why, but seeing it made my stomach heave.

"I couldn't sleep," Charlotte was half whispering. "I put on my robe and came in to get a book, and there he was. I thought he'd fallen asleep, so I shook him and—and he just sort of fell over. Is he . . . ?"

I nodded. There was no sign of what had happened, but there was no mistaking that Jeremiah Boyle was dead.

Gingerly, I stepped closer. On the carpet to the right of

Boyle's chair was a book of music with a dark blue cover. Evidently Boyle's head, in falling forward, had dislodged it. I didn't touch it or even bend over to look at it, but I didn't have to. I knew what it was. The Jacobi edition of Rameau's works for harpsichord.

"What time is it?" I asked stupidly.

Jackie pointed to the wall clock. "Four thirty-five."

What to do next? I cudgeled my weary brain. "We have to get the captain."

"Don't leave me," said Charlotte. "I mean, I'm all right, but . . ."

"You and Jackie go," I said. "I'll wait outside."

Sudden awareness brought Charlotte's hand to her mouth. "Oh, God. Kitty. She'll have to be told."

"Go ahead," I said.

Seconds after they'd disappeared, a door opened down the passageway. Feuerman, in his denim shorts and Lacoste shirt but barefoot, came padding toward me. He looked sleepy and irritable. "What's going on? Is something wrong?"

"We've got a big problem," I said.

"Why? Is somebody hurt? Get out of my way, for Christ's sake." He tried to push past me into the salon.

I put a hand on his chest and shoved him back, none too gently. "The captain will be here in a minute. I think we'd better wait for him."

"Who the hell do you think you—" He stopped. Jackie, Charlotte, and Hayward were hastening down the passageway. Behind them were several people, including one or two crew members, in various stages of sleepy disarray. Cabin doors were opening and heads were poking out to find out what was going on. But the particular person I was watching for wasn't anywhere around.

Hayward, looking surprisingly fresh and very official, stepped between Feuerman and me with a brisk nod. We trailed him into the salon. The others hung behind.

"Jerry? Good God, Jerry!" Feuerman gasped.

Hayward went up to the body, lightly touching the

outstretched hand and squatting on his heels for a brief look at the face and chest. He rose and took off his cap in an odd little gesture of respect.

"He's gone. And he's been shot. I want you all out of here. I'll have to radio ahead to the police."

"Shot? *Shot?* Bullshit. Let *me* look."

"Now, Mr. Feuerman, I can't let you do that." Hayward spoke in an apologetic drawl, but his arm was like an oak beam barring the way. "What I'm going to do is seal off this room. Eddie!" He called over our heads to one of the crewmen. "Eddie, go get Carl, will you?" Carl, he explained, was his first mate. "He's a good man, and reliable. Some of these others, why, hell, you wouldn't believe—Mrs. Feuerman, I wouldn't come in here right now. Stop her, somebody."

But it was too late. Kitty pushed her way past Hayward with surprising strength and came up to Boyle's body. She stared at it wordlessly, then put out a finger to touch Boyle's shoulder. "Jerry," I heard her whisper hoarsely. "You're gone. Hello, Jerry, and good-bye."

"Kits . . ."

"It's all right, Charlotte. But one strange thing. I thought I heard somebody say Jerry was shot, and of course that isn't true. It isn't, is it, Everett?" She turned to me. "You. You seem to know things. You can tell me it isn't true, can't you?"

Hayward had the diplomatic answer. "Mrs. Feuerman, as soon as we find out what happened we'll let you know."

"All right. But people shouldn't go around saying those things. I mean, they might think that I—"

"No, they shouldn't," Charlotte interrupted her. "Now let's go."

As soon as the two women had left the room, Feuerman said to Hayward, "Listen. If Jerry really was shot, you ought to secure that rifle of yours."

"Funny you should mention that," said Hayward. "I always keep that gun locked up, and the ammo too. Because—"

"Captain," I cut in. "I've got another question. Where's Ray Gerard?"

"Isn't he here?" Hayward craned his neck to peer at the half dozen people in the hallway. "Guess not. Well, you're right, that *is* strange. He's supposed to be Mr. Boyle's security man, and I always thought he was pretty good."

"Maybe somebody ought to go look for him," Feuerman said.

"Whoa, now, one thing at a time," said Hayward. "Carl, come on in here." Sunburnt, wearing khaki and a slightly wise-guy expression, Carl looked like a twenty-two-year-old version of Hayward, only a good deal dumber. "You probably know by now, Mr. Boyle has been shot," Hayward told him.

"You serious, Skip?" He caught sight of the body, did a double take, and swallowed hard. "You're serious, all right."

"It's what I'm saying. Now, we're going to all get out of here. What I want you to do is lock those doors to the fantail."

"Don't do that," Feuerman said.

"Why not?"

"Fingerprints."

"Yeah," Hayward said, "that's right. Could be finger-prints all over the place. Okay. Carl, then, don't mess with anything. We're going to shut these doors. You just take this chair over here and move it right outside and sit in it, and don't let anybody go in the salon. Got that?"

"Yessir, Skip, sure do. Nobody gets in."

"If anybody tries to get in, you let me know, hear?"

"Yessir, I sure will."

Hayward stood in the doorway and faced the handful of people outside. "I guess you all know what's happened. Mr. Boyle has been shot and killed. But there are folks still asleep who don't know. What I think we better all do is get together upstairs in the dining room at"—he looked at his watch—"five thirty. That's in about twenty minutes. That will give everybody a chance to get up and get dressed and braced up to the bad news. I'll get the galley boys to get some coffee organized. Any questions? No? Okay, see you up above."

Hayward hurried off to his bridge and radio. His departure served as a kind of signal to the rest of us to disperse and start spreading the word.

We were in Ralph and David's cabin, waking them to tell them the news, when we heard a single low cry of pain. It stopped almost at once and was followed by utter silence.

"Kitty knows. That was Sally," Jackie said.

Mistress and mother. I shivered with a midwinter chill.

We roused Terry, and Jackie and I went back to our cabin to dress properly. The five of us together went upstairs to the dining room.

Captain Hayward had been better than his word. An urn of coffee was waiting, and plates of pastries as well. We gulped the hot liquid gratefully and waited. A few at a time, various members of Boyle's party appeared. Nobody made any conversation. After about five minutes, Hayward walked in. He was just about to start speaking when the door opened and Everett Feuerman and Charlotte Sensabaugh came in and took seats. Kitty Feuerman was between them. She was calm, but there were dark stains under her eyes and her shoulders were rigid with strain. Only Sally Boyle was missing. No, I was wrong: Sally Boyle and Ray Gerard.

"Folks, I guess you all know what's happened. About an hour ago, Jeremiah Boyle was found in the salon. He was already . . . deceased, when Mrs. Sensabaugh found him. She ran for help to Mr. and Mrs. French of the musician group, and they went with her to check and then alerted me. I've had a look at Mr. Boyle. It appears that he was shot in the chest. I did not see any gun."

There was a stir in the room. Nobody said anything, but Kitty shook her head slowly. In disbelief? In denial? I couldn't tell.

Hayward was speaking again. "Now, you all understand that we have to comply with the law in this terrible situation. I have radioed the Turks and Caicos authorities and they have ordered me to proceed with all possible speed to Grand Turk Island, where the police will come on board. We'll be there by midafternoon. They also ordered me to seal off the salon, which I have done. Nobody is to go in or out of there.

"Finally, I suggest that for your own safety and convenience you not move about the vessel alone. If you go to your cabins or staterooms, make sure you lock your doors."

"Captain, are you suggesting that there's some kind of . . . murderer running around loose, and that we're not safe?"

"I'm not suggesting anything, Mr. Feuerman. But it's a fact that Mr. Boyle was shot, and that's a police matter. I'm simply passing on the recommendations of the folks on Grand Turk."

"Well," Feuerman barked, "what have you done to locate the one individual aboard this vessel, as you call it, who habitually carries a gun?"

"Captain Hayward!"

We spun around in our seats. Sally Boyle was standing very erect in the doorway. She looked stricken and her voice was not quite steady, but her competence and authority were undiminished. "Is there someone here who knows first aid? I have found Mr. Gerard on deck, and he is hurt."

"I do. I've been a nurse." Lawyer Shaver's girlfriend Christine jumped to her feet amid a buzz of talk.

"I'll go too," Terry said. Terry, I remembered, had taken EMT training in case anyone eating at Monza's choked on the bistecca alla finanziera or went into cardiac arrest over the fettucine Alfredo.

In the end, everybody crowded out of the dining room behind Sally Boyle and her two-person rescue squad. Sally led us along the deck to the deserted spot where, from Jackie's account, Boyle had made his pass at her. God, could that have been just the day before yesterday?

Anyway, there in a deck chair was Ray Gerard. His head hadn't flopped forward like Boyle's, but was tilted back against the top rail of the chair. His eyes were closed, and as we stood there he slowly wagged his head from side to side and groaned. It was easy to understand the groan. Somebody had clouted him behind his right ear, hard enough to raise a big bruise and draw blood.

"Don't touch him," commanded Christine the ex-nurse.

Terry stared her down, knelt beside the deck chair, and took Gerard's wrist in his hand. "It's okay," he said, "you're gonna be okay."

"Oh, if you want to do that, it's all right," Christine said. Terry ignored her.

Gerard grinned weakly and seemed to relax in the chair.

"His pulse is normal," Terry said after a moment. "He's concussed, naturally, but it's not too bad. You want to get him inside, we can probably move him right in the chair."

"With a head wound?" Christine said. "There's no way."

"I feel like such a jerk," Gerard said painfully.

"Take it easy, baby," Terry said; then he said to us, "You know those sandbags we had for the concert? If they're still around—"

"Oh, if you can immobilize the head, that's different," Christine said.

A crewman was sent for the sandbags. Terry set them in place, one on either side of Gerard's head. Three of us picked up the deck chair with Gerard in it and carried it safely to the nearest cabin. It was Sally Boyle who opened the door and switched on the light.

While Christine stood by giving orders, Terry himself eased Gerard onto the bed.

"I never even saw the son of a bitch," Gerard said, wincing.

"Hey," Terry said, "wouldn't you be a lot more comfortable without all of that hardware?"

"Yeah, I guess so," said Gerard. He waved his right hand feebly in the direction of his chest, then gave up. He was really not in the best shape.

Terry reached gently under his blazer and slipped Gerard's stubby-barreled revolver from its spring holster. "Here you go. Where do you want it?"

"Put it by me . . . pillow. Don't worry . . . safe."

"He shouldn't have a gun right by his ear like that," Christine said.

"*You* try to take it away from him," Terry said.

"S'okay," Gerard said groggily. "S'safe. Jus' wanna go to sleep."

"I ought to look at that cut first," Christine said.

"It's stopped bleeding, it looks clean and his color's good," said Terry. "If it were up to me, I'd let the guy sleep. But you're the doc."

Christine stood indecisively by the bed. "I guess you're right," she said finally. "I'll stay with him, though."

"My dear, do you have pencil and paper?" Sally Boyle asked. The girl nodded. "If he says anything about who struck him, or about anything else that matters, do write it down. It could be very important."

"Okay, Mrs. Boyle. But what about you? Shouldn't you be lying down, too?"

Sally actually managed a small smile. "No, thank you, I'm perfectly well. I've never been one to take to my bed and weep when trouble comes."

CHAPTER 12

*E*ven as Sally spoke we heard a winch start up and a clatter of chain. *Enchantress* was weighing anchor. A minute later, with a deckhand still hauling the swimming stage inboard, the engines came on and we headed slowly out of our cove, a holiday craft no longer.

"If you'll forgive me," Sally said, "I do want to go back to my cabin. There will be calls to make and family to notify, and with Mr. Gerard out of commission I think I had best begin the planning."

"If there's anything at all," Jackie said.

"I'll let you know, of course I will," Sally said with that ghost of a smile.

"May I at least ask them to send you some tea?"

"Yes, please, my dear, how considerate. Only not tea, please, coffee. A pot of good strong Jamaican coffee. I'll let you in on a secret. I detest tea."

"And to think the poor thing has had to go to teas all her life," Jackie said later.

We'd ordered Sally's coffee and acquired a pot of our own. We'd taken this, sought out Ralph and David, and settled in a sheltered spot on deck to watch an uncomfortably bloody sunrise.

"Thank God none of this has anything to do with us," I sighed.

"If you believe that, lovey, you'll believe anything," Ralph said.

"I don't get it," I said.

"He means you're a suspect," said Jackie.

"Oh for Pete's sake," I said.

"No, listen to me," said Ralph. "Didn't the late Mr. Boyle go for Jackie in a big way?"

"I guess he did, but it wasn't exactly in a big way. It was more of a reflex action. Or so Jackie and I thought."

"Sure, but he didn't just make goo-goo eyes, did he? He made a grab."

"He certainly did," Jackie said. "I've got a bruise on my shoulder to prove it."

"You said you banged it on the cabin door," I said. "If I'd known it was Boyle, I'd have killed the so-and-so."

Four pairs of eyes fastened on me in silence.

"There you go," Terry said triumphantly. "He could have done it. He had a motive. Jealousy."

"It's only a little bruise," Jackie said helpfully.

"But men have swung for less," David intoned.

"What's *wrong* with you people?" I said.

"We're not just being heartless, Alan," Ralph said. "The police are going to be asking you about this, don't think they won't be, and you need to be ready."

"What do I say?" I said. " 'I would have murdered Boyle if I'd known he'd hurt my wife, but I didn't know so I didn't murder him'? Terrific."

"You can say you were with me the whole time," Jackie said.

"Somehow I don't think the cops would take your word for it," Ralph said. "Not without a lot of other evidence."

"Get serious," I said. "Granted I'm a suspect because of Jackie, it seems to me there are plenty of better suspects."

"Who, for instance?" Ralph said.

"Well . . . I suddenly didn't like the idea of nominating people I'd met and socialized with, even nasty ones, to the post of murderer. "Obviously, Kitty Feuerman for one," I offered. "She'd qualify."

"On jealous mistress grounds," Ralph said.

"Exactly. Then there's Everett Feuerman."

"How do you figure him?" Terry asked. "He knew Boyle was making it with his wife and he didn't seem to give a damn."

"Maybe he was secretly bitter about it," said Jackie. "Maybe he harbored feelings of jealousy and resentment."

"That iceberg?" Terry asked. "Never."

"He certainly can shoot," Ralph added.

"Yeah, well, so can other people," Terry said, "like that guy Williams, who was popping at the fish before Feuerman."

"You mean Williamson," I said. "He missed, don't forget."

"But that doesn't mean he can't shoot," Terry insisted.

"This isn't making any sense," I said. "Feuerman, Williamson, Sensabaugh, Shaver—they were all in this bank deal with Boyle. Boyle was their ticket to a whole lot of money. Why kill him before the deal was finished?"

"Maybe the deal wasn't going so well," David suggested.

"That's possible," I admitted. "I don't think Feuerman, Williamson, and Sensabaugh are on the same wavelength at all, but the thing is, Boyle seemed to have them under control. And I think the deal was under control too. From what I heard yesterday, they'd worked out a very slick strategy to persuade the bank people to sell. So why kill the goose that lays the golden eggs?"

Nobody had an answer to that.

"And while we're at it, what about Ray Gerard?" I asked.

"We *know* he carries a gun. He seems like Boyle's faithful old retainer, but maybe Boyle had said or done something that, while I'm talking in clichés, broke the camel's back."

"I can tell you one thing," said Terry.

"What's that?" Ralph asked.

"Gerard's gun. I got a good look at it when I pulled it out from under his coat, and a good sniff at it too. There were bullets in all the chambers and no smell of powder. I don't think it had been fired recently."

"He may have six other guns, for all we know," I said.

"You've made your point," Ralph said. "There are other logical suspects. But that doesn't rule you out."

"I didn't do it," I said, "honest I didn't."

"I feel awful," Jackie said abruptly.

We all stared at her. The sea was perfectly calm, and *Enchantress* was cutting through it as smoothly as a warm knife cuts through butter. "If you have to be sick," I said, "let's go below and get it over with."

"No, idiot," she said, "it's nothing like that. It's Boyle. It's horrible enough that he's down there dead. But I have this hideous feeling that what's *going* to happen now will be even worse."

"You mean the investigation?" Ralph asked.

"Yes," she said slowly, "and the way people will behave."

"With this crowd," Ralph said, "you could be right."

Within the hour, the first evidence was in.

I'd gone down to our cabin to get our sunglasses, and on the way back I bumped into Williamson the banker—I mean literally bumped into him. He was charging down the passageway, briefcase in hand and his mind a million miles away, and he banged right into me.

"Oh Jesus, I'm sorry," he said, "I'm late for a meeting." And then, "Christ, this must be terrible for you people."

"For us? At least we didn't know him well," I said. "It's got to be much more terrible for his friends and family."

"Yeah, sure, of course," Williamson said. "It's an awful thing. Awful. But we're not going to let it stop us." He stood straighter, poked out his chin, looked determined, and jiggled his briefcase. "We've just got to regroup and move ahead."

I decided to play dumb. "Move ahead? With what?"

Williamson became elaborately casual. "Oh, things. But what I really meant was we simply can't let this get us down. Jerry would be the last person to want that."

I nodded and mumbled something meaningless, and we parted. In fact, I couldn't wait to get away. I had no doubt what that meeting of his was about, and the knowledge was making *me* feel a little awful too. These great pals of Boyle's clearly weren't going to let a little thing like Boyle's getting murdered interfere with their forty-million-dollar bank take-over.

"Well, and look at it from their point of view," Ralph said unconcernedly when I described the encounter. "Why should they back off? There could be a lot more in it for them if they can pull off the deal with Boyle out of the picture."

"So maybe one of them did take Boyle down after all," Terry said, "to sweeten the pot."

"Maybe they all did it together," was David's contribution.

"We're talking about a bunch of businessmen and politicians," I said, "not about crack dealers or Hell's Angels."

"Stranger things have happened," Ralph said.

"I guess I should feel relieved," I said. "At least you've decided that I'm not the number-one suspect."

"I wonder what the Grand Turk police are like," Jackie said to change the subject and keep the peace.

"We'll find out soon enough," Ralph said cheerily.

According to the literature in the cabin, *Enchantress* cruised at twenty knots. That's brisk for a pleasure yacht. But long before lunchtime we were tired of sitting on deck and watching the shoreline crawl by.

There was no real lunch, just sandwiches and coffee, which was just as well. None of us felt like facing a roomful of Boyle's friends and having to wonder with every mouthful which one of them had killed him.

The only good thing that happened was that Christine the ex-nurse appeared on deck just after noon and told us that Ray Gerard seemed much better. "I got his shoes off," she announced, "and then his jacket and tie, though not that awful shoulder holster, and he even made a joke about being undressed by a pretty girl. But he said his head hurt too much to take advantage of the opportunity and then he fell asleep."

"Did he say anything about who might have clobbered him?" Jackie asked.

"No, not a word, and I didn't ask. But anyway, he probably doesn't remember."

It's not clear in my mind what we all did to kill time for the sad remainder of our voyage.

Terry and David wanted to go on with their Chinese checkers tournament, but the Chinese checkers were locked up with Boyle in the salon, so they had to make do with Terry's deck of cards. Jackie buried her nose in a book. Ralph leafed through the pages of an ancient issue of *Town & Country*. He said it was the only publication in the world that made him immediately want to join the Communist Party and hasten the revolution, but what could he do? His alternative reading material was a book called *How To Get Along With Your Cat*.

I tried various dodges. I worked out programs for concerts. I thought about applying for a Guggenheim to study the music of a southern Mediterranean country starting next January. I wondered what it would be like if Jackie and I had a baby.

At three fifteen exactly *Enchantress* nosed her way into a tiny harbor and tied up at the town wharf of Cockburn Town.

None of us quite knew what to expect. Squad cars and paddy wagons filled with cops, guns at the ready? No, this was a Crown Colony; it would have to be shiny black Jaguars with oval rear windows and blinking orange lights, carrying broad, stolid men in raincoats, all of them looking like the late Jack Hawkins.

What we got for starters was two bobbies—I had no idea

whether that's what they were called, but they were dressed like bobbies and wore the same tall hats with shiny silver badges—plus one man in a seersucker jacket, blue shirt, club tie, dark gray Bermuda shorts, snappy gray below-the-knee socks, and shiny loafers.

There was plenty of time to absorb all this detail of dress because the minions of the law closed in on *Enchantress* with the speed and determination of molasses.

I remarked on this to Terry, who has relatives on the force.

He looked at me as if I were mentally retarded. "Why should they be in a hurry?" he demanded. "Cops never hurry unless they have to. This is a tiny little island. They know we're not going anywhere."

We watched from a safe distance as the gangplank was lowered and the three men strolled aboard. Hayward was there to greet them and escort them below. It seemed so friendly and harmless: the master of the vessel showing around one more party of visitors. But the thumping of my heart was a reminder that it wasn't harmless at all.

Five minutes later a door opened and both bobbies came out onto the boat deck and went ashore. One of them seated himself on a bench a few feet from the gangplank. The other hurried off down the street.

"That cop's not a guy," David said.

He was right. The face under the second bobby's helmet wore the detached look the police cultivate the world over, but it was definitely not masculine. Trust David to spot a woman anywhere.

In a few minutes, the female bobby was back with a large black leather valise.

"Aha!" said Terry the expert.

"What's aha?" Ralph asked.

"That's for the camera, the chalk, the fingerprint stuff."

The next arrival drove up in a little red car, which he left parked carelessly on the grassy strip between the street and the wharf. A short man with a clever cheerful face and a pointy nose, he exchanged a few words with the bobby doing guard duty on the bench, walked on board, and went below. He too was carrying a black bag, a small one.

"Gotta be the M.E.," Terry said. Even I knew he meant the medical examiner.

We heard a discreet whimper from a muted siren. An ambulance drew up behind the medico's car. One of its two white-clad attendants pulled an empty gurney out of the rear compartment and used his foot to propel it across the grass. Its wheels rattled lightly on the cleats of the gangplank. Once it was on deck, they picked it up and carried it through the door.

There was quiet for about ten minutes. Then the female bobby reappeared. She opened the door and held it open. The two attendants came through, rolling the gurney carefully. One at each end, they eased it down the gangplank. Straps kept the load from slipping. With the weight on it, its wheels made no noise at all.

Once the men had the gurney on shore they slid it quickly inside the ambulance. One of the attendants made a note on a clipboard and put the clipboard in with the body. He shut the rear door and walked around to get in beside the other attendant, who was already behind the wheel. The engine made almost no noise as they drove off.

With the midafternoon sunlight hot on my back, I shivered.

"What's the matter?" Terry asked. "You feeling sick, like Jackie?"

"Not sick," I said, "scared."

CHAPTER 13

ow then, ladies and gentlemen, let me introduce myself and my colleagues. I'm Detective Chief Inspector Benjamin Nye, that's spelled N-Y-E and pronounced as in very close indeed."

The few of us who caught the feeble little joke smiled halfheartedly. Nobody felt like laughing.

"My senior associate here is Detective Sergeant Philip Peto. Our junior associate, the lass on my left, is Detective Cathy Sproul. Call me Chief Inspector, call Phil Peto Sergeant, call Cathy Detective Sproul and you'll be on the right track."

It was so incongruous. Here we were in *Enchantress's* dining room on a beautiful afternoon, listening to a lecture on how to address the police.

"What we're here to do is to inquire fully and carefully into the sudden unexpected death of Jeremiah Boyle."

Something about Nye's intonation set off a faint tremor of doubt in my mind. You're paranoid, I told myself, ignore it.

"Our preliminary examination indicates that this unnatural death may well have been a crime. It appears that Mr. Boyle was struck, and very likely killed, by a bullet fired from a gun. A weapon has been found in the vicinity of the body."

"It has?" I whispered to Jackie. "Where? I didn't see any gun."

"Shhh."

"Under these circumstances," Chief Inspector Nye went on, "the law clearly lays down what must happen next. A postmortem procedure will be performed by Mr. Edgar Rosegarden, our police surgeon, who is also a fully qualified pathologist. We're extremely lucky to have him here in the islands."

Kitty Feuerman's fists closed and opened again.

"The postmortem findings will be communicated to a jury at a public proceeding known as a coroner's inquest. Those of you who read detective novels with a British setting will no doubt recognize the term."

Jackie the thriller fan nodded. I grinned at her and she wrinkled her nose at me.

"Before the forensic evidence is given, those with knowledge of the unfortunate event will be asked to tell the jury under oath what they know. It is the job of the police, you understand, to conduct interviews to gather this testimony. We shall be doing so starting at once. And," Nye added smoothly, "to help us in our examination of the physical evidence, we do have to have everyone's fingerprints."

"Oh *Christ!*" Everett Feuerman said in a strangled voice.

"Is that a problem, sir?"

"Oh, no, not in the way you're thinking, Chief Inspector. But some of us are very upset. My wife, for instance, and Mrs. Boyle. I mean, my God, you're not going to have to fingerprint Jerry's—Mr. Boyle's *mother*, are you?"

"Don't be so foolish, Everett," Sally Boyle said in her low

clear voice. "Of course they must take my fingerprints, and yours, and everybody's."

Feuerman muttered something under his breath but said nothing more out loud.

"Thank you, ma'am," Nye said. "Now, all of this is going to take some time and cause some inconvenience, we know. We could ask you to stay here aboard the yacht, but you'd probably find this rather confining. So we've made arrangements to accommodate you ashore. We've nowhere fancy to put you, I'm afraid, but I think you'll find the two guesthouses we've selected quite comfortable."

"Excuse me, Chief Inspector," said Hugh Shaver, "but can you give us any idea of how much time you plan to take? We of course want to cooperate in any way we can, but . . ."

"If I knew, I'd be happy to tell you. But I think you must assume several days at least. Of course, you're free to move about the island when we're not actually in need of your assistance."

Shaver whispered behind his hand to Sensabaugh and Feuerman. "Thank you," he said to Nye.

"I think that's about it for now," Nye said. "If you'll all queue up at the table in the back, we can get the fingerprinting started. And we'll want to talk to some of you straightaway after that, before we send people ashore. But I do want to urge any of you who have knowledge that might be helpful not to wait for us, but to come forward at once. Any questions? Right, then, let's carry on."

Detective Cathy Sproul was in charge of the fingerprinting. "Hello. Name, home address, and phone on the card, please. Roll your fingers slightly on the pad and press, not too hard, good, now the thumb, good, now the other hand, good, thank you. Oh, Mr. French?"

"Yes?"

"You're one of the people Chief Inspector Nye would like to see this evening."

"Me? What for?"

"I expect he'll tell you that. He's holding court in the

room where Mr., um, Boyle was found." She consulted a list. "You know where that is. Why don't you go down there in about half an hour?"

Uneasily, I waited out the interval on deck with Jackie and the others. I told myself not to be stupid, that I hadn't done anything to feel guilty about, but even so my legs were rubbery when I walked in the salon door.

The harpsichord was still in place, but everything else in the salon seemed to have been picked up and put down somewhere else. The police at work, obviously. I was fascinated to see not chalk marks but shiny red tape marking the spot on the rug where the Jacobi Rameau had been.

Sergeant Peto was using the card table as a desk. He had both a tape recorder and a notebook in front of him. Nye was half sitting, half sprawling on the sofa. At closer range, he was tireder and more battered-looking than I'd thought. His opening words caught me completely off guard. "Christ," he said, "you Yanks. What a mess."

I gaped at the two of them.

"Sit down, sit down," he said, waving a hand at a chair. "Try not to look as if you were swallowing flies. You're Alan French?"

"That's right."

"Good. You're the head of a musical group the deceased hired to play for himself and his guests on this cruise?"

I explained who we were, how we'd come to meet Boyle, what sort of music we played and all the rest.

"Thank you, I'm sure that will be very helpful," Nye said. He sounded bored. "Now suppose you tell us what you know about what happened last night."

I told him it had been a long hard day and that we'd been happy to get to bed. I told him about being asleep and dreaming and waking up to hear Charlotte Sensabaugh's banging on our door and calling out that something had happened to Boyle. And about going down to the salon with Charlotte and Jackie and finding Boyle's body.

"And that was it, eh? You knew he was dead."

"Yes," I said. "I remember thinking you couldn't be mistaken about it. He *looked* dead. Of course, I had no idea he'd been shot."

"I see. Then what happened?"

I told him about sending Jackie and Charlotte to fetch Captain Hayward and about holding off Feuerman until they'd all arrived. "After that, Hayward closed off the salon and posted somebody outside, and we went back to our cabin and got properly dressed and went up to the dining room."

He asked me about time.

"It was four thirty-five when we—Jackie and I—first saw the body. I know because I asked what time it was and she pointed to the clock on the wall. So it would have been a few minutes earlier that Mrs. Sensabaugh woke us up."

Nye grunted. "Jackie. Jackie is your wife?"

"Jacqueline Craine French. She uses Jackie Craine professionally."

"But the two of you are legally married?"

"What do you mean, are we legally married? Of course we are," I said. "What's wrong with you? You want to see our marriage certificate?"

My outburst seemed to be just what he wanted. "Now, Mr. French, please. No offense meant. I just wanted to make sure."

"Well, you've made sure."

"Mr. French, your wife is an attractive woman. Would it be fair to say you are devoted to her?"

"You bet it would," I said.

"Would it be fair to say that you would be jealous of any approach to her by another man?"

There it came, the million-dollar question, big as life and twice as nasty. I knew I could be in deep trouble, and yet for some bizarre reason the situation struck me as funny. "Absolutely," I said, "and not only that, it's a certifiable fact that Jerry Boyle did make a pass at Jackie, a very physical one, and later hung around sort of leering at her in a nice polite Ivy League way. But it's also a certifiable fact that he got nowhere. The first person Jackie came to, right after this . . . approach, was me. And we discussed it after that with the other members of the group."

"Your musical group, the Antiqua Players?"

"Right. Because we thought Jackie's being upset might affect our playing."

"And when did all this supposedly take place?"

"It didn't 'supposedly' anything, it *did* take place. The day of our performance. The day before yesterday. Right before lunch. But what I'm really saying, Chief Inspector, is that, sure, I was mad at Boyle, he was being a pain in the ass, but I had no reason to kill him. Punch him in the nose, maybe, but kill him? Don't be ridiculous."

"No reason?"

"None whatsoever."

Nye stared at me. If he was trying to intimidate me, he succeeded. "Mr. French. You're not being completely candid with us, you know."

That really threw me for a loss. "Sure I am," I said, "why wouldn't I be?"

"I have no idea, I'm sure. But why haven't you told us that your wife was up on deck early this morning, rather, er, lightly clad?"

I couldn't help it. I burst out laughing.

"That strikes you as funny?"

"It *is* funny. Jackie couldn't sleep. She woke me and said she was going up on deck to look at the stars. I remember telling her to watch out, Boyle might be waiting, or words to that effect. She was gone about five minutes. And as for being lightly clad, as you so charmingly put it, she had on a flannel bathrobe and rubber flip-flops, so if you're suggesting that she was all ready for a big sex scene with Boyle, you're being ludicrous."

"And how do we know that what you're telling us is the truth?"

"I suppose you don't know," I said. "I can't *prove* it. But ask Jackie. Ask any of the others in our group. I know, I know, it's my wife, they're my friends, so naturally they're going to cover up the fact that I'm a killer type. Or ask Mrs. Sensabaugh. We talked with her about Boyle's love life, or whatever you want to call it, quite extensively yesterday afternoon."

Nye and Peto exchanged glances.

"Now, Mr. French," Nye said, "would you mind taking us through the chain of events once again?"

"Starting when?" I asked.

"Why not start at the point when you went to bed?"

So that's what I did. This time, I filled in more detail. For instance, I remembered to tell them about finding the Jacobi edition of Rameau on the carpet near the harpsichord. "I guess he'd been practicing his Rameau."

"Why was that, do you think?"

I had to tell them then about Boyle's corralling us to hear him play, and the aftermath.

Nye nodded. "That seems to explain one thing, at least. Boyle told his mother sometime last evening that he was going to stay up to practice, that he'd been given quite an inspiring critique by members of your group."

Inspiring. I'd have to tell that to Jackie and Ralph. It sounded so much like Boyle.

We went through the rest of my story the second time and then I had to start all over again at the beginning, but finally Nye pronounced himself satisfied. "I think we've grilled you enough for now," he said with a sardonic smile. "The sergeant will type up his notes and the tape into a statement, and later we'll ask you to read it over, make any corrections, and sign it."

"When will that be?" I asked. "Sometime tomorrow?"

"It will if the bloody typist doesn't turn up sick," Sergeant Peto rumbled.

"Mr. French, before you go . . ."

I eyed him warily.

"This is an unofficial question and you don't have to answer it," Nye said. "But off the record, have you any idea what went on on this cruise of yours to make somebody want Jeremiah Boyle dead?"

"Does that mean I'm not a suspect?" I asked hopefully.

Nye stiffened. "No, it doesn't mean that at all. It means that I'm asking you, as a favor if you like, to give me a bit of background. If you know any."

If the chief inspector wanted me to do him a favor, maybe I'd better do him one. "Well, it's no secret about Boyle and Mrs. Feuerman. That they were . . . close, and that they had quite a quarrel going."

He nodded. Evidently he'd already heard it from somebody else.

"Then there's this business deal," I said.

"What business deal?"

I told him what I knew about the bank buy-out and named the principal players. I didn't say anything about eavesdropping on a strategy session. Maybe I should have, but I didn't.

Nye's eyes gleamed. "Interesting," he said thoughtfully, "in fact, fascinating. Swain's Bank, eh? You know, they're about the biggest employer on these islands. But would that give any of the people on your boat reason to murder Jeremiah Boyle? Rather the reverse, I should say."

"Me too," I said, "but these are the only two situations I know anything about."

"All right, Mr. French, thank you. You've been most helpful. I think we'd like to talk to Mrs. French next."

"I'll go get her for you."

"It wasn't really too awful," Jackie said afterward. "They wanted to know all about my little tête-à-tête with Boyle, so I told them. They asked me who else I'd told and I said, well, Alan, of course, and then Ralph and Terry and

David and Charlotte Sensabaugh, sort of. Did I miss anybody?"

"Nope."

"And then I said that when I told you, you became inflamed with jealous rage and you picked up your revolver that happened to be lying there and—"

"Oh fine. I understand that some prison systems allow spouse cohabitation for long-term offenders."

"Spouse cohabitation," Jackie said dreamily. "Mmm. Sounds nice. Well, anyway, what I really said was that I couldn't *stand* Jerry Boyle but that you hadn't murdered him out of jealousy and I hadn't murdered him out of battered-woman syndrome and that they should stop being silly."

"You really said that?"

"Really and truly."

"And did they believe you?"

"I think so, but I'm not sure. And oh, yes, they asked me what I was doing wandering around the deck in the middle of the night and I told them. And they asked me what I was wearing and I said my bathrobe and flip-flops."

"You Jezebel," I said. "Prowling the night in search of—well, in search of Boyle was what the cops seemed to be thinking."

She laughed. "In that tacky robe? I've had it since I was fourteen."

"That's never stopped *me*. But seriously, what did you think about Nye and his questions?"

Jackie picked up a brush and began brushing her hair. She gives it a hundred strokes a day, every day, rain or shine. "He came after us right away," she said more or less intelligibly as she worked, "because we're musicians . . . and not rich or influential . . . but they know . . . we didn't do it . . . and so now they're stuck . . . ninety-nine, one hundred. But they did tell me one thing."

"What was that?"

"The inquest is day after tomorrow."

Just as she spoke, there was a rap on our cabin door.

"Yes?"

"It's Carl, sir. The captain says to please pack your bags. You'll be moving to the Sea Salt Guest House in about half an hour."

CHAPTER 14

The Sea Salt was painted pink with white trim. At the rear of its shady garden were three cottages, also pink and white, each with a tiny flagstone terrace overlooking the sea. The police drove us there from the waterfront, a matter of about three blocks. The management put Jackie and me in one of the cottages, Ralph, Terry, and David in another, told us when dinner would be served, and left us in peace.

It took Jackie about three minutes to unpack and two more minutes to settle in with her gamba.

I was stretched out on an ancient wicker couch, listening and feeling the stress wrinkles in my forehead begin to smooth themselves out, when somebody began tapping persistently at the front door.

"Damn," Jackie said, not looking up.

"I'll go." I levered myself up and went.

The woman might have been in her midtwenties. She

might even have been thirty. But there was no question about her looks. Nice tan, not a lot of makeup, expensive tasteful clothes with plenty to admire under them, tiny gold and sapphire earrings in pierced ears. Regular features, maybe a little too regular, intelligent blue eyes, determined executive-type mouth and chin. "You're Alan French, aren't you? They said cottage three. I'm sorry to interrupt, but may I come in?"

Jackie stopped playing.

I was in no mood to be gracious. "And who might you be?"

"Naturally, nobody would have told you," she said, sounding amused, sarcastic, self-assured, and upset all at once. "I'm Lauren Winship."

The economist. Boyle's other girlfriend. "Okay, come on in."

"I have to talk to someone," she said. "I went down to meet the boat and there was a policeman there who said there had been some trouble, that Jerry . . ." Her control lapsed momentarily. "That Jerry Boyle was *dead*. Is it true? Was he really . . . ?"

"Sit down, Ms. Winship," I said. "Yes, it's true."

"Oh God," she said, "that bitch. How could she?" She took a pretty beige handkerchief from her Vuitton carryall and pressed it delicately to the inner corner of each eye. Curiously, I detected real shock and sadness in the gesture. Maybe it was even more genuine for being so disciplined, Lauren Winship's response to grief.

"I don't know who you're referring to," I began.

"Oh, Alan, don't," Jackie said, "she's just upset."

"Have you got a tissue?" Ms. Winship said.

Jackie handed her one and she blew her nose once, hard. "I'm sorry," she said more normally, "coming here like this and doing this. It's not the way I generally behave. But the police were so vague, and they wouldn't let me on board, and they said Ray Gerard was sick and couldn't see me, and—and I knew your name from Jerry, and I knew that you were just there for . . ."

"Entertainment value," I suggested.

"Well, anyway, that you weren't, that you wouldn't be *involved*."

"And you thought Alan might be a good person to tell you what happened," Jackie finished up.

"That's right. And I have to know," she said with intensity. "I can't function otherwise."

"How did you find out where we were?"

"The policeman told me that they'd moved people into guesthouses, this one and the Turk's Head. I'm staying here, I've got cottage one, so I asked here first. Now, please tell me. What really happened? Was there a big fight?"

"Wait a minute," I said. "How do you I know you are Lauren Winship and not a reporter for the local rag or a stringer for *The Miami Herald*?"

She reached into her carryall and handed me her passport.

I glanced at the photograph and handed the passport back to her. "Okay, Ms. Winship, you're you. Yes, I guess you could say there was a big fight. But big fights don't necessarily end in killings."

"No, they don't," she agreed.

She composed herself and listened while Jackie and I gave her the bare bones of the story, from the lunchtime quarrel to the discovery of Boyle's body and Ray Gerard's head injury.

"God," she said when we finished, unconsciously echoing Chief Inspector Nye, "what a mess! What a horrible mess. And maybe nobody will ever know who was responsible."

She sat for a while without speaking. Then she said quietly, "How ironic. Jerry is—was—a real bastard. He could afford to be, and he was. But I wanted him. He was so *elegant*, you know? And this was to be when it happened. He was coming here to tell *her* that they were history. I mean, that's what he told *me* he was going to do. Now I guess I'll never know whether it really would have happened or not. Oh well, *sic transit* I guess." She used her handkerchief again, just as

127

carefully as the first time. Then she said, in quite a different voice, "Did you know they were all coming down here to buy a bank?"

"We'd heard something about that," I said cautiously.

"Do you know if they're still going to try to do it?"

"Ms. Winship," I said, "I really don't know. But Hugh Shaver is staying here in the main house. You could ask him."

"Hugh? Oh good. Thank you. And thank you for being so forthcoming and understanding." She was just getting to her feet when there came another rap on the door.

"Now who's there?" I called out.

"Me." The door opened and David walked in. "Hi," he said, and then he caught sight of Lauren Winship. "*Hi.*"

"David Brodkey, Lauren Winship," I said. "David is our lutenist."

"How fascinating!" she said, sitting back down.

"Ms. Winship was a good friend of Jeremiah Boyle's." David looked sadly at the floor. "Oh. Gosh. I'm sorry." Lauren Winship nodded sadly back. "Thank you."

"What's up, David?" I asked.

"I was just wondering what you were going to do about dinner."

"I don't know. Eat here, I guess."

"Okay. Excuse me," he said a little belatedly in Lauren Winship's direction. "I didn't mean to interrupt."

"You weren't interrupting anything," she said. "I was just on my way out. But if you're wondering where to eat"—David gave her his shy small-boy inquisitive look—"there's a wonderful little seafood place on the harbor. In fact, I was going to eat there myself. I won't be such great company tonight, I'm afraid, but if you don't mind . . ."

"Gee, that does sound good. I love seafood. Would you guys mind?"

"Not in the least," I said. "Feel free."

Lauren Winship thanked us again and said she was sure we'd be seeing each other often. To David she said, "Why don't we meet in front in about half an hour?"

They went out our door together as if they'd known each other all their lives.

"It's the tropics," I said. "Relationships ripen fast."

"I'll say," said Jackie, picking up her bow again.

From what we'd seen of Lauren Winship in action, we weren't too surprised to find her sharing a table at breakfast the next morning with Hugh Shaver and Atley Sensabaugh. She looked up when we walked in and gave us a polite hello. Then she went back to what she'd been doing, drawing diagrams with a Cartier roller marker on the tablecloth and explaining them to her companions. Briefcases and yellow legal pads were much in evidence among the coffee cups. David was nowhere in sight.

"Business after pleasure," Jackie murmured as we seated ourselves and had a go at the melon.

"Poor David," I said, "playing second fiddle to forty million dollars. He won't be used to that."

"Maybe it won't happen."

When David did come in a few minutes later, he sat with us. Lauren, we were pleased to see, waved and smiled with enthusiasm. After breakfast, it was David, not Shaver and Sensabaugh, who walked her into the garden. But just before lunch the two gentlemen just mentioned drove off with Lauren in a taxi. All three of them, I noted, were dressed for success.

Charlotte Sensabaugh came to the doorway to watch this exodus, her lips pressed tightly together. "Do you know who that was?" she demanded when she saw Jackie and me.

I said I did.

"Do you know what she's done? The nerve of her! She's talked Atley and Hugh and Tommy and Everett into going ahead with this business with the bank. And it's just *hours* since Jerry was murdered in cold blood!"

"Wait a minute, Charlotte," I said. "I know you can't

stand Lauren Winship, but you have to be fair. They were going ahead with the deal anyway."

The annoyed look on her face gave way to a you-can't-fool-me smile.

Explaining how I'd found out about this supposedly hush-hush decision didn't change Charlotte's mind one bit, or her expression either. "Maybe they were going ahead, but *she's* a party to it. And one more thing," she snapped. "If I don't tell you, nobody will. That nice young man in your group, the one who plays the lute, now she's after *him*. I hear they had dinner last night and spent the night together. What do you think of that?"

"Good gracious me," I said, "how shocking."

She got my message. "I knew it. I knew you'd think I was nothing but a gossipy bitch. But you have to warn your friend about her before it's too late. It makes my blood *boil* to see her carrying on as if nothing had happened, when Kitty—"

"How *is* Kitty?" Jackie asked.

Charlotte looked both puzzled and distressed. "You know, it's the strangest thing. She's barely said a word since she found out. Of course, she's been under sedation much of the time. But she did go and speak to the police. That Inspector Nye. I have no idea what he asked her or what she said, but it was obviously terrible for her. She came back and went straight to her room. I must say they sent a car.

"I know she's not talking to Everett. He's always so impatient with her, and, anyway, he's all tied up with business. Business as usual, that's Everett. But what I can't understand," she almost wailed, "is why she won't talk to *me*. I mean, I'm her best friend."

Jackie and I did our best to reassure her, and after a while she said that talking to us had made her feel better and she thought she'd go for a walk on the beach as she'd been planning to do.

We said we thought that would be relaxing, and we headed off toward the center of town, which lay in the opposite direction.

"She's basically nice," said Jackie. "But . . ."

"She's enjoying herself a little too much?"

"Exactly. And the idea that we should warn David."

"Hee hee hee," I said.

"Men are absolutely disgusting," Jackie said, "but you're right."

We spent a couple of hours wandering around Cockburn Town. There wasn't that much to see, but the sun shone, the ambience, as they say in the guides, was full of charm, and we were grateful to be able to stretch our legs. Even coming across the impressive stucco creation that housed police headquarters hardly tightened my nerves at all.

More impressive still was the main office of The Bank of Samuel Swain, Ltd. on Front Street. You name it, Swain's had it: marble paving, steel and glass facade, atrium garden, fountain, copper sculpture, restored historic sailing craft, fish-motif murals by local artists.

"It's great," I said. "It's so rich you practically can't tell it's a bank. Looks more like a progressive school."

The ensuing discussion, which somehow drifted from contemporary architecture to private versus public education for small children in New York City, lasted us all the way back to the Sea Salt.

We made it there none too soon. Minute by minute as we walked, the sky darkened. What had been a pleasant breeze became a chill damp wind. A sprinkle of rain caught us as we hurried through the garden. By the time we were inside, it had settled into a steady semitropical downpour. We needed Jackie's small folding umbrella to get from our cottage to the main house for dinner.

David flashed us a damp grin as we made our way through the little lobby. "I won't be eating with you tonight either. Lauren says the pizza at McGonigle's is wonderful. See you later."

I doubted it.

Ralph and Terry did join us, though, and after the usual ten-minute Antiqua Players exercise in indecisiveness all four of us ordered the seafood platter the waiter swore was the gourmet delight of the islands. It was a serious mistake. Halfway through the main course, our waiter came back to our table. "Look out," said Terry, "now he's going to promote some horrible dessert." But instead, the waiter announced, "Miz is wanted on the telephone."

"Me?" Jackie asked.

"You the only lady here."

She came back a few minutes later, frowning. "It's the police. They want me to come to headquarters."

"Now?" I asked, "in the pouring rain?"

"They say come right away, that it's important. I guess I'd better go."

"I'll go with you," I said.

"Don't be silly, Alan, it's just down the street. You finish your dinner and I'll meet you in the lounge for coffee." Before I could argue, she excused herself and left.

A couple of minutes later, I said, "You know, something about this doesn't feel right."

"I agree," Ralph said. "We shouldn't have let her go by herself."

"Tell you what," said Terry, "why don't I call the cops and ask for Jackie?"

"Okay," I said, "but while you're doing that I'm going down there after her."

I got up and went to the front door. It was still raining steadily, but less violently than before, and it was dark, so dark I had to wait on the doorstep for my eyes to adapt. As soon as they had, I set off down a Front Street empty of traffic toward the center of town.

Twin yellow globes lit the entrance to police headquarters. The light they threw was blurry, so until I drew near I couldn't make out more than the indistinct outline of the person who was standing in the doorway. It was Jackie. She hesitated at first, then walked quickly toward me. "Alan, is that you?"

"None other."

"Thank goodness!" She came up close and grabbed my arm. "Listen. Something very weird is going on. The police say they never called me at all."

"You're kidding."

"No, I wish I were. I talked to the woman at the desk and she didn't know anything about it. She checked with criminal investigation—they're the detectives—and the person there didn't know anything about it either."

"Jesus Christ," I said.

"But that's not all. I'm not sure, but on my way here, I think somebody tried to do something to me."

"What do you mean, do something?"

"I was walking along pretty fast, the way you do in the rain, and all of a sudden I heard something go kerchunk on the pavement about ten feet away. Something big and heavy. And I felt something sting me on the cheek. I looked around, but I couldn't see or hear a thing. So I just took off. I practically ran the rest of the way here."

"I don't blame you one damn bit," I said. "What else happened? Did you tell the cops?"

"No. I mean, I didn't really know what *to* tell them. I waited inside for a long time, though. I was scared. I was thinking of calling a cab when I decided I'd look outside to see if you might be coming. And you did come." She laughed a little shakily and clutched my arm tighter and my heart turned over in my bosom with worry and love.

"Come on," I said, "we can't stand here all night in the rain. And no matter what you think, we have to report this."

Jackie looked dubious, but she went back with me into headquarters.

The bored-looking black policewoman behind the desk gave Jackie that what-you-again? look. She listened while I explained what we thought had happened. With many lickings of the thumb to turn pages and many pauses to get our names right, she made a note of the incident in a big ledger. Then she told us that there was no way they could investigate tonight. "They only three of us here, you see, and we needed in case of emergency." It seemed to me that dropping a heavy object on or near my wife's head might constitute an emergency, but what I thought didn't matter. "You come back later," the policewoman said, later meaning tomorrow.

Could we use her phone to call a cab?

"Pay phone in the hallway, but the cabs be all gone home." She was right. We had to walk. I wasn't exactly thrilled by the prospect.

"This is the place," Jackie said, stopping in front of a large house six or seven down from the Sea Salt. "I mean, I think this is the place."

"You think right," I said. "Look."

A yard away in the streaming gutter lay a block of pale stone. It looked rather like a curbstone. That is, it was about two feet long, six inches wide and six inches thick. A chunk was missing from one corner. Instinctively, I glanced at the curbing nearby. It was unbroken. "It must have been dropped from up there."

We peered up into the rain, but even though light was coming from the upper windows of the house, we could see very little. The roof in particular was wrapped in shadow.

"At least I'm not imagining things," Jackie said.

"You sure aren't," I said. "Somebody lured you out here and flung that thing out of a window or off a roof. Either they wanted to scare you or . . ."

"But why?"

"I can't imagine. But it must have something to do with Boyle's murder."

Under Jackie's umbrella, we splashed our way very slowly back in the direction of the Sea Salt and hot showers and Band-Aids—Jackie had a slight cut on one cheek—and restorative drinks. Even though there wasn't another soul in sight, I made us walk right down the center of the road.

CHAPTER 15

The nicest thing about Chief Inspector Nye's office was Chief Inspector Nye's executive swivel armchair, complete with high back and overstuffed tufted Naugahyde upholstery. The chair Nye kept for visitors was neither nice nor overstuffed. It was a bare wooden object as functional as a gibbet. I wriggled uncomfortably on it and listened to what Nye had to tell me. I liked that even less than I liked the chair.

"We *have* investigated, Mr. French," Nye said with elaborate courtesy. "Quite thoroughly, in fact. The most likely explanation of what occurred is that it was simply an accident. Our constable went to the spot you indicated on Front Street. He didn't find the stone you described—"

"Of course not, twelve hours later," I scoffed.

"—but your description is consistent with the type of limestone we use here as roofing. Constable Dent went to the trouble of checking the roof of the nearest house. Evidently a piece of roofing tile was loosened by last night's rain and fell to the street near Mrs. French. That's not the sort of thing we like to have happen, and we've spoken to the homeowner, but there's very little more we can do."

"And the phone call that brought her out in the first place—was that an accident too?"

Nye shifted in his chair, which creaked beneath his weight. An evasive look, you might even have called it a foxy look, spread over his face. "The phone call, yes. As you've been told repeatedly, we know nothing about the phone call. If you had any idea who might have made it . . ."

"All Jackie knows is that it was a woman's voice with a French accent."

"Creole, Mr. French, in all probability. Many Turks Islanders speak Creole. We do a good bit of trading with Haiti. But to finish what I was saying, if you had any notion of who might have made the call, we could proceed. Impersonating a police officer is something we take seriously."

Just in time, I stopped myself from asking why in that case he didn't arrest himself. "The long and the short of it," I said instead, "is that you're not going to follow up at all."

"Put yourself in my place, Mr. French," Nye said patiently. "Try, anyway. We have fourteen detectives to cover this entire two-hundred-square-mile patch. Our number-one crime problem is drug smuggling and keeping the stuff away from our own people. Our number-two problem is money laundering arising from drug smuggling. Our number-three problem is killing arising from problems one and two. But tiny little problems like these aren't enough. To make our life really complete, in comes your lot on a charter yacht with a dead body on board, and the death turns out not to be accidental. And now you're demanding that we stop everything to track down a hoax phone caller."

"But that's just it," I protested. "The phone call and the attack on Jackie must be related to Jeremiah Boyle's murder."

"Maybe they are," said Nye. "How?"

"How the hell would I know?" I said, losing patience. "Maybe the murderer thinks Jackie saw him that night. Or knows something about him."

Nye looked at me for a long time. There was no friendliness in his gaze, but neither was there animosity. It was as if he were sizing me up, asking himself if I were someone he could say things to. "You know," he said finally, "this investigation is going to take a very long time. I don't doubt it will turn out to be the most complicated case I've ever handled. We've next to no physical evidence, and what we do have is contradictory. The victim was a man of influence. His family and friends are powerful sophisticated people. Their business and governmental connections in the islands are very good indeed." He paused. "As for you and *your* friends . . . I suppose I shouldn't tell you this, but I can't see any real involvement there, either."

"Thank you for that," I said. "But you're not trying to imply that Boyle killed *himself*, are you? Or that he died of that well-known natural cause, getting shot?"

"No, I'm not saying either of those things."

"Well, then, don't you have to look into what happened to Jackie?"

"Mr. French, I understand your concern. But even if you're right about it not being an accident, this, er, mishap of your wife's is only one small part of a much bigger case. Given our limited resources, we're pushing ahead as hard as we can. As hard as we can." Nye rolled back his chair in token of dismissal. "I hope you appreciate our position."

"I guess so," I said, rising to go.

"We'll see you at the inquest tomorrow."

"Close your eyes and *think*," I said to Jackie.

"I have thought, over and over again. There just plain isn't anything to remember. I left our cabin, I went up the stairs—"

"Companionway," I said.

"Aye-aye, Horatio Hornblower, companionway. I didn't see anybody when I was going up on deck, I didn't see anybody when I was *on* deck, and I didn't see anybody when I came back down."

"I didn't know you liked C. S. Forester," I said.

"I have many hidden dimensions," said Jackie.

I kissed her.

"Don't interrupt. I do like C. S. Forester, especially when he makes Hornblower play whist for a living. It's a lot like what we have to do for a living. Furthermore, I am a very observant person."

"Amen to that," I said.

"The reason I didn't see anybody, darling, is that there was absolutely nobody to see."

"I wish the guy who dropped the roof thing on your head knew that."

"Me too. But, Alan?"

"Yes?"

"What makes you think it was a guy?"

"Place your right hand on the Bible that's it sir do you Alan French solemnly swear to tell the truth the whole truth and nothing but the truth so help you God?"

I was the sixth witness.

Of the first five, only Ray Gerard had shed any new light on the case at all. Looking none the worse for wear except for the neat beige bandage behind his right ear, Gerard had identified the pistol found on the floor near Boyle's body, a .32 caliber Beretta, as Boyle's own gun. The reason I hadn't seen the gun, it turned out, was that the book of Rameau's music, which I *had* seen but hadn't touched, had fallen on it and hidden it.

I'd waited expectantly for somebody on the jury to ask Gerard about his own ordeal, but nobody had, and Gerard himself hadn't volunteered anything. Evidently Nye was determined to keep the lid on tight.

By the time I took the stand, the small mob in the whitewashed courtroom had long since stopped coughing and popping its gum and had fallen entirely under the soothing spell of routine. The coroner, a plump man in bright plaid Bermudas, had introduced himself at the outset as Josiah Durfee. Mr. Durfee invited me to tell my story in my own words. That took about three minutes. He then called for questions.

A male juror asked me if I'd seen a nude masked man with a revolver running along the deck, since that was one of the rumors going the rounds. I blinked and said I hadn't.

Another juror, an elderly lady in a flower print dress, raised her hand and was duly recognized. "Mr. French, while you were in that room, could anybody have been hiding *inside the harpsichord?*"

This bit of ingenuity produced a buzz of excitement, which was promptly gaveled silent, as well as a gratified smile on the face of the juror. I smiled too. Hercule Poirot, move over. I was genuinely sorry to have to explain to the lady that because of the way harpsichords are built there wouldn't have been enough room in Boyle's harpsichord for even a very small murderer.

"Are there any more questions?" Mr. Durfee asked the jury.

Nobody else raised a hand.

"May I say something?" I asked. "Last night—"

"The witness is reminded that he is here to answer questions about a homicide, not to make statements," Mr. Durfee said in stentorian tones. He'd obviously been warned to head me off if I tried to bring up what had happened to Jackie. "If there are no more questions, the witness may stand down."

"But—"

"The witness may stand down!"

You can't win 'em all. I stood down. Half an hour and two witnesses later, the jury retired. Half an hour after that, it returned to deliver a verdict of "death at the hand of a person or persons unknown," and to be thanked for its pains and dismissed along with the witnesses.

"What was that all about?" I asked a neatly turned-out young man who'd been sitting a few seats away. We'd just emerged from the Law Courts into the bright sunlight. I felt frustrated and used up, all at once. The cheerful resort props, the lush lawns and colorful flowers seemed to mock the barren exercise we'd just been through.

"It means that Nye doesn't have a clue," the young man said. "He doesn't want to close the case and catch hell for not doing his job. But he also doesn't want to push on with it and catch hell for that. He can reopen it if anything turns up. Which it won't," he added mournfully like Eeyore in *Winnie-the-Pooh*.

"Why won't it?" I asked him.

"Oh, the usual reasons. Overworked force, rich, important people, offshore jurisdiction. But hold on!" The young man interrupted himself, brightening and slipping a notebook and ballpoint out of his jacket pocket. "You were going to tell the jury something, weren't you? Something about last night. What was it?"

"You're a reporter?"

"Teddy Barringer, *Conch News*, at your service."

"Now, now, Mr. Barringer, no badgering our witness." Chief Inspector Nye edged his bulk between the reporter and me. His smile was jovial but his eyes were not.

"He's not badgering me," I said. "But is there really a *Conch News*?"

"Oh yes," Nye said. "Comes out every week. Like spots."

"There's a *Turks and Caicos News* too," said another voice. Its owner had a red face, a red waistcoat, and a cock-of-the-walk strut. "We'd like to talk to you as well."

Jackie tugged at my arm. I knew perfectly well why. She didn't want me to get Nye's back up. Talking to the press was clearly one way of doing just that.

I decided that a modicum of tact was called for. "Look," I said to Barringer and his competitor. "Why don't you run over to headquarters and check out the blotter or the complaint sheet or whatever it's called for last night."

"Is that all you can tell us?" Barringer wanted to know.

"Apart from that, my lips are sealed."

"All right," the other reporter said. "Thank you very much." He sounded less than pleased as he and Barringer departed, but that might just have been my tender conscience.

"Now you've done it," Ralph said with a laugh. "How about, 'Boyle Mystery Witness Nixes Comment on New Violence'?"

"Nah," Terry said. "It'll be more like 'Yacht Beauty Hubby Says, "Boyle Killer After My Wife."'"

"Don't you guys have anything better to do than think up phony *Daily News* headlines?" I asked.

"That's just it," said Jackie, "we don't. The sooner we get out of this mess, the better."

On the way back to the Sea Salt we spotted the eatery called McGonigle's and decided to sample the pizza Lauren Winship had praised so highly. We avoided the house specialty, pizza with conch and bonefish, and stuck to the more mainstream product. "A nice effort," was Terry's verdict, "but I guess Lauren what's-her-name comes from someplace that's, you know, nonjudgmental about pizza. Like Cleveland, or Omaha."

In the next breath, Terry made up our minds for us about what to do with the rest of our afternoon. "What do you mean, you feel funny going to the beach? Boyle's dead, but not going to the beach will bring him back, is that it? Come on, get into your suits."

So we toasted ourselves on the sand until Jackie said it was long enough after the pizza to swim, and then we swam and toasted ourselves some more and Ralph, with us as kibitzers, started construction on a serious sand castle.

Forty-five minutes later, Ralph, the tip of his tongue sticking out of the corner of his mouth, was using a seagull feather to put the finishing touches on the steps of a circular staircase.

"Can you really make the stairway go through both arches?" I asked.

"Yes."

"And up into the main turret?"

"Just watch. Do *you* think they'll ever find out who did it?"

"No," I said.

"No," said Jackie.

"I doubt it," Terry said. "What about you?"

"There," Ralph said. He'd fashioned a tiny banner out of the tip of the feather. He stuck it gently in the conical roof of the turret, sat back on his heels, and dusted the sand from his fingers.

"It's beautiful," Jackie said. "I never knew you could do that."

"Thank you, lovey. It is nice, isn't it? I don't agree with you all. I think they *will* find out. I think this Boyle business is a long, long way from being over."

Waiting for us at the Sea Salt was an unexpected visitor: Ray Gerard. With a shrug and his usual thin smile, he accepted our congratulations on his speedy recovery.

"I'm okay," he said. "Got a hard head, I guess. Of course, I can't remember a damn thing about getting slugged. But the worst I feel now is dumb."

Much to my surprise, Gerard was philosophical about his professional lapse. When we said how sorry we were, he became quite forthcoming. "I'll tell you folks the truth. I was with the man fifteen years as his personal assistant. Before that I was with his father. Sure, they knew I was Bureau, that's why the old man hired me. He wanted an accountant who could carry, and I don't just mean carry figures." He smiled reflexively: it must have been an old joke.

"I had you down for Fordham Law," I said.

"That too. I have both. I did my CPA while I was still with the Bureau. Anyway, I went with the Boyles mostly to handle the checkbook, keep an eye on investments, check out contacts, that sort of stuff. It shades over into security, I grant you that, but they didn't expect me to do bodyguard work. We have other people we use for that. Besides, on a boat trip like this with nobody but friends and well-wishers like yourselves, what kind of security problem is there? Maybe the boat sinks, is all.

"The thing of it is, this is very inside work. The way I look at it, we could've had an army out there, it wouldn't have made any difference. Do I feel bad? Of course. I feel lousy. You didn't know Mr. Boyle like I did, and in a lot of ways he was a great person, a great individual. But was this my fault? I don't see it. I don't have any guilt. Not that I wouldn't love to get hold of the son of a bitch who did it."

"You think that will ever happen?" I asked.

He shrugged. "Who knows? I hope so. Anyway, that's not what I came over for. The first thing, let me give you this." He handed me a sealed envelope, just as he'd done after our concert at Boyle's house. "That's your fee. The next thing is to get you out of here. We've made reservations for you on the morning Pan Am flight to Miami tomorrow. In case you want to hang around Miami, you've got open tickets from Miami to New York."

"I'll take the tickets," Jackie said.

"The last thing, Mrs. Boyle especially asked me to thank you for playing and for everything else you've done."

"How is she?" I asked.

"She's fine," Gerard said. "In fact, believe me, she's really remarkable. There's more. She wants me to say that she'll be in touch soon, she won't forget. She won't, either."

We sent back our thanks and best wishes. I said I'd write.

Before Gerard left, he insisted on shaking hands with all four of us. "Tell that other little guy I'm sorry I missed him. And tell him to go real easy with the ladies. That one he's fooling around with right now could spell trouble with a capital T."

"That other little guy" turned up just as we were going in to dinner. David elected not to tell us how he'd spent *his* afternoon and we didn't ask him. He did agree, however, that McGonigle's pizza looked better than it tasted. As for our dinner, nobody can really do much for frozen chicken breasts in cream sauce except label them suprêmes de volaille à la Normande, but then nobody can really do much *to* them, either.

We had the lounge to ourselves after dinner and were dawdling over our coffee when bang! the door flew open and in charged the Swain's Bank buy-out brigade, shedding jackets, dropping briefcases, loosening ties and collars and baying for strong drink.

"You guys must have had a rough afternoon," said Terry.

Feuerman grunted. Sensabaugh snatched his rum concoction from the barman's tray and downed two-thirds of it at a gulp. Williamson stared morosely at the salted peanuts. Shaver gave that Doberman bark of a laugh of his. Only Lauren Winship, smiling at David over her white wine and soda, seemed reasonably satisfied with life.

Feuerman helped himself to a heaping plateful of the Sea Salt's special cold curried shrimp. "I don't understand them," he complained between mouthfuls. "I don't understand them."

"Shut up, will you, Everett," said Sensabaugh.

"Oh shit, A.R.," Shaver said, "these characters already know everything anyway."

Feuerman finished his shrimp and turned his attention to his second double martini. "I don't understand them," he said again. "The money is right. We're telling them they can all keep their jobs. The whole board can stay on. We've even offered to up the directors' fees. But the silly bastards are frozen like rabbits. They won't go forward and they won't go back."

In the silence that followed, Lauren Winship got up from the table with her drink and came across to share a sofa with David. He grinned and put an arm around her. Then he did something outrageous. Even I was startled. He addressed Feuerman exactly as if the man were a colleague. "That's no big problem," he said, and he added five more words that I couldn't quite hear.

Feuerman set down his drink. His face darkened and his bushy eyebrows drew together in a memorable frown. He glared across at David and took a deep breath. I was sure he was about to blast David off the face of the earth, when he suddenly stopped short. "Say that again," he commanded.

"All I said was, Take something away from them."

Again there was dead silence.

A distant, distracted look appeared on Feuerman's face. After a long, long time, it was followed by the beginnings of a broad smile.

"I'll be goddamned," breathed Sensabaugh. "I think the kid's got something."

"What is it that they think they have that we can take away?" Williamson wondered aloud.

"Anything. Everything. Who cares?" Feuerman said. "The point is, we've been giving, giving, giving. They think they can sit there and raise the ante forever, but now is the time to shatter that illusion. Hugh, call them, will you? Set up a meeting for first thing tomorrow morning. Tell them we have one more proposal to put before them, a very generous one. We'll have some dinner and go straight to work."

Feuerman signed the tab and the four men grabbed their jackets and briefcases and left the room.

"David, that was great," Lauren said, "but I'm sorry, it's going to break up our evening." And she too picked up her briefcase and disappeared.

"'I could not love thee, dear, so much,'" Ralph misquoted reflectively, "'Loved I not money more.'"

By seven the next morning, Jackie, Ralph, Terry, and I were waiting with our bags and instrument cases for David and *his* bags and instrument cases, so that we could all get into the two waiting taxis for the trip to the airport. Our flight was due to leave at eight, and the airport was only ten minutes away, so we knew we had plenty of time.

At seven ten, we called David's room. No answer.

At seven thirteen, we sent Terry to David's room to wake him up.

At seven seventeen, Terry came back to report that David's bed had been slept in, but that at present David wasn't in it. Nor was he in the john, the shower, or anywhere else in the vicinity.

At seven twenty-two, David appeared. Just David. No bags, no lute in its case. "I'm a little late," he said shamelessly. "I've been kind of busy."

"David Brodkey," Jackie said sternly, "here is your airplane ticket. Here is two hundred dollars. We're rehearsing the day after tomorrow at five o'clock. What you do between now and then is your own affair. But don't *dare* be late for that rehearsal!"

"No, Jackie, I won't, I swear."

"And get the lowdown on the bank deal," I added.

At seven twenty-nine, the rest of us started back to New York.

CHAPTER 16

Whoever said getting there is half the fun is a fucking liar," Terry said between his teeth.

It was four thirty in the afternoon, the ghastly hour when according to some nutrition guru I've read, the blood sugar count bottoms out and body and mind are most vulnerable to depression. A chill rain was dribbling down, bringing with it all manner of vile acids, chemical wastes, and particulates from the factories and dumps of the Garden State. At the moment, we were temporary residents of the Garden State, but if the dearth of buses and taxis at Newark Airport went on much longer, our status would change: we'd be New Jerseyites forever.

Like a distant memory of happiness, the thought of the canceled nonstop from Miami International to LaGuardia lived on in my mind.

"We're really better off taking cabs." I resumed the

argument with our treasurer. "The limo will dump us in midtown and we'll have to take cabs anyway."

Our treasurer sneezed. "We can take the subway," she said.

"Jackie, by the time we get in, it'll be five thirty on a Friday afternoon. Rush hour. We'll be crushed to death."

"I don't care," she said. "We'll die *warm*."

"There's a cab!" Ralph screamed. "Two cabs!" He flung himself off the sidewalk, elbowing the gentleman with the Seeing Eye dog into the traffic stream and overturning a stroller and its little passenger, but winning the race for one taxi and making the other slam on its brakes to avoid instant demolition. He and Terry heaved their stuff into the frontrunner. "We'll call you later!" Terry shouted and they were off in a cloud of greasy spray.

What foreign land our driver thought we were from, I can't imagine. He started off on the right foot by informing us that the fare from Newark to New York City was two hunnert and twelve dollars. Unfortunately for him, he let us into the cab first.

"Oh, how nice," Jackie cooed, signaling me to lock both doors from the inside so we couldn't be dispossessed. "Would you please drive us to Twentieth Precinct headquarters? That's at Eighty-second, between Columbus and Amsterdam."

"Aw shit, lady, you don't really want to go there."

"For two hundred and twelve dollars, we do," she said sweetly. "For some other price, we might go somewhere else. Might you have some other price in mind?"

He might indeed, surprise surprise: the meter charge plus tolls plus ten bucks for a total of about thirty-five dollars, the tip to depend on future good behavior.

Jackie's grasp of New York City reality so impressed the driver that he actually helped unload our luggage and hump it into the lobby. We were grateful for his aid, neither Incarnación the primary doorman nor Ramón the super being anywhere around. We made known our gratitude in dollar terms, so despite our unhappy start we and the cabbie parted good friends all around.

The front elevator was working, which is not always the case. It took us up to the apartment and I unlimbered my doorkeys, one for the regular lock, one for the police lock, one for the dead bolt. Everything inside was as usual. There was the familiar faint odor of gas from the kitchen, mingled with the familiar not so faint odor of the horrible stuff the exterminator uses to sustain our fragile truce with the roach empire. There was the jumble of music stands and the shelves of scores and records. There was Jackie's cactus, which dislikes me intensely and thrives in my absence out of spite.

Jackie, still in her raincoat, put her arms around me and hugged me. "We're home. Did any of it really happen?"

"Try asking Jeremiah Boyle that," I said. Then I quickly said I was sorry, that wasn't funny, it wasn't funny at all.

While Jackie was unpacking, I clattered around in the kitchen making us a cup of tea. We sat on the sofa in the studio to drink it.

"We played so well," Jackie said sadly.

"Sometimes it turns out that way," I said. "You like to think music is magic, that playing well makes people like Boyle better people, that it makes the world a better world. But sometimes all music is is consolation."

"You know, you're right," she said in a surprised voice. "Thank you for your words of wisdom."

"That's me," I said. "Guide, philosopher, and friend. More tea?"

"Yes please. Look at all this mail!"

"I am looking. Do we need a six-foot-high genuine porcelain Chinese garden bench?"

"Of course we do. How about the world's best electronically balanced rowing machine? Or here's something: a complete home tool kit designed exclusively for women, over seventy separate tools in a handsome fitted briefcase for only three hundred dollars."

"Just say no," I said. "And throw out the catalogues."

Over the next few days, the usual nutty New York whirl caught up with us. Our first spring concert was one week away. Jackie was running to keep up with a book full of private lessons and master classes. Ralph had The Barn and a daily forty-five-minute subway commute to Brooklyn Heights, where he was directing a Bach cantata for a gay men's church group. Terry was working at Monza's and giving flute lessons. I had to pick out a violin for one of the brattiest twelve-year-olds in New York and also practice for a Baroque String Ensemble concert coming up the night after our own concert in the wilds of Staten Island.

As busy as we were, at odd moments images of Jeremiah Boyle and what happened aboard *Enchantress* kept popping into my head. Sometimes I saw Boyle slumped over the harpsichord, sometimes it was the great fish, bleeding in mid leap. But most often, it was Jackie. Jackie in closeup, her face intent, at the concert. Jackie at a distance, standing in front of the police station in the rain. Always, of course, the same questions. Who had killed Boyle? Why? Of all the motives his killer might have had, which was the one that had triggered the act?

I hadn't yet reached the stage of dreaming about Boyle's death, but it was never very far from my waking thoughts.

David showed up for rehearsal as promised, disappeared for a few days—we all figured he was hiding from Simone—and surfaced in time for the concert and the modest group feast at Pino's that followed. "Look what Lauren gave me," he said between mouthfuls of wood-oven pizza and diet soda.

"Lauren? Lauren Winship?" Jackie said. "When did you have time to see her?"

"She's out in Cleveland right now," he said evasively, "but look." He handed me a tattered bit of paper. It was a five-day-old clipping from the Midwest edition of *The Wall Street Journal*. The headline read DESPITE DEATH OF PRINCIPAL, BOYLE SYNDICATE PROCEEDS WITH ACQUISITION OF PICTURESQUE CARIBBEAN BANK.

The story led off with the word that a syndicate formed by the late Jeremiah T. B. G. Boyle of New York had acquired a majority interest in The Bank of Samuel Swain, Ltd. The syndicate's members were named: Feuerman, Williamson, Sensabaugh, Shaver, one or two people we'd never heard of, and yes, Lauren Winship. The exact purchase price wasn't cited, but "sources close to the transaction" estimated that it was between thirty-five and forty million dollars U.S., which I thought was impressively close to the figure I'd overheard.

Everett Feuerman was quoted as saying that the syndicate had voted to proceed even though its organizer, sadly, had met death on a cruise "under circumstances that have yet to be unraveled." The acquisition, Feuerman added, was "too beneficial and too far-reaching to be abandoned, even in the face of tragedy."

"The man has a terrific way with words," I said.

Terry's verdict was briefer and different: "What bullshit."

There followed a brief biography of Boyle and a paragraph on the history of Swain's Bank, which dated back to the beginnings of the salt trade in the eighteenth century.

The story ended with the terse announcement that Everett Feuerman had been elected chairman of the bank's board, replacing Sir Samuel Swain, who had been named head of the finance committee.

"I guess Feuerman did okay for himself," said Terry.

"Sounds like they all did," I said. "Lauren too."

"She didn't tell me what she got," David said.

"Maybe she didn't want to scare you away," said Jackie.

"She wouldn't scare me," David said fervently.

We laughed.

Ivor Rhys is Jackie's manager. When Ivor called the next day to, as he said, "lunch her," I urged Jackie to hold out for Bellini's, but she said Ivor said Bellini's was overpriced and crowded and anyway only fat tenors ate fegato di vitello alla Venezia and how about some really great sushi?

Ivor wants Jackie to do a big tour. Jackie wants Ivor to take on the entire Antiqua Players. Neither party really wants to do what the other party wants, but Ivor is a gifted manager and he's been great for Jackie, so she said okay to no Bellini's but finally talked him into La Boîte en Bois on West Sixty-eighth.

"What's wrong?" I said when she came in. "Too much butter in the puff paste? Ivor give you grief?"

"No," she said in an odd voice, "nothing like that. It was what happened after lunch. I ran into Kitty Feuerman."

"No kidding," I said. "And how is Kitty?"

"Strange," Jackie said. "Wow, was she strange. The first thing she said when she saw me was, 'I've been looking for you all over New York. I *must* see you.'"

My heart began to beat faster. "And?"

"I tried to tell her how busy we were. But she just said, 'Oh, surely you can spare me an hour. An hour, that's no time at all. What about tonight?'"

"Tonight? What did you say?"

"I hemmed and hawed, naturally, but of course it was no good."

"So you made a date with her for tonight. Where?"

"Someplace called the Russell, on Fifth in the Seventies. At nine o'clock."

"I'm going with you," I said.

"I didn't think there were still places like this in the world," Jackie said in a hushed voice. I knew what she meant. The bar of the Russell had floral carpeting and walls paneled in dark, dark mahogany. The sconces on the walls shed light so discreetly that you could scarcely see your partner across the table, let alone identify anyone else in the room. Two or three elderly waiters padded about in the dimness with drinks on silver trays. The few customers were exclusively solitary middle-aged women, their small elegant purses on their tables, their fur coats draped protectively around them. They must have been too lonely to drink at home.

"What's *he* doing here?" Kitty Feuerman said when she saw me. She didn't wait for an answer, but instead signaled a waiter. "Bring my friends a drink, and I'll have another as well."

The waiter bent over stiffly to take the order. "That's two white wines and a vodka martini, madam?"

"No," said Kitty, with the sudden cautiousness of the heavy drinker on the verge, "three white wines."

"Very good."

"Isn't this *charming*?" Kitty said. "So quiet. So private. Just the place for lovers. Or ex-lovers. Or what am I? A widowed lover, I guess. If there is such a thing. I suppose the two of you are lovers. Well, then, you'll know what I mean. It's a great atmosphere."

"We're in love," I said. "But we *are* married."

"Oh really," Kitty said without interest, "I didn't know. Anyway, I didn't bring you here to talk about love. I brought you here to tell you things. The first thing is, I didn't shoot Jerry. You probably think I did, jilted mistress and all that, but I didn't."

"I don't think anybody thinks that, Mrs. Feuerman," Jackie said.

"Kitty, you must call me. You're very sympathetic, you know. I can tell that about people, it's one of my things. That's why I had to see you. Charlotte was right about you. You're a lovely person. But oh yes, some people think I did it. They don't say anything. They wouldn't, of course. But they think it all right. But never mind all that. The other thing I want to tell you is, the one to watch out for is Ray Gerard."

"But why?" I said, mystified.

"Did you know he killed a man once? Just shot him in cold blood. You ought to find out about that. And Ray Gerard knows everything about Jerry's business. Everything. Who knows what kind of a secret thing they had that went wrong? And also, he's jealous. Jealous of anybody he has to share Jerry with. Why," she cried, "he was jealous of *me*."

Jackie and I stared at each other, dumbfounded and distressed.

"If that's true . . ." I began.

"And not only that," Kitty overrode me, "I don't think he was hit on the head at all. I don't care what Sally says. I think he was acting. You find out about him. I must go now. Everett will be home from the office and he'll be upset if I'm not there."

Mechanically, I asked her how Feuerman was.

She gave a little laugh. Her voice sounded more relaxed, almost normal. "Oh, Everett. Men are so funny. The other night he came in from a late meeting. I thought he'd be happy—he's head of the bank now, you know. I even said something to him, congratulated him. But he just looked right through me. He was the same way the night Jerry was killed. I was eating dinner in our stateroom and he came in and I said, 'Congratulations on your deal,' or words to that effect and he didn't even smile.

"But Everett's fine. And I'm fine. Don't you worry about us." Again her tone changed. Her eyes gleamed in the dimness. "You look like pretty good detectives to me. You go find out all about Ray Gerard."

"Does she really believe what she's saying?" I asked Jackie at home later.

"I can't tell," Jackie said. "She's obviously so messed up, she wants to lash out at everybody and everything, and yet she's terrified of what would happen if she did it herself. I suspect she does know something bad about Ray Gerard, though."

"What I'm wondering," I said, "is whether she didn't dish out all that stuff about Gerard to cover up something else she knows."

Jackie nodded. "Like who really pulled the trigger. I wondered that myself. But who would she cover up for? Her husband?"

"I doubt it. But what about her roommate?"

"Charlotte? Can you see Charlotte murdering anyone?"

"I frankly hadn't thought about it," I said. "But she was

the first one on the scene, remember. It would have been easy for her to pretend to *find* Boyle dead when actually she'd made him that way."

"That's sick," Jackie said. "And anyway, why on earth would Charlotte do it?"

"It's funny," I said, "but Kitty herself gave us the motive. She was talking about Gerard, but it applies to others as well."

"What do you mean?"

"Jealousy. The original green-eyed goddess."

Jackie gazed at me thoughtfully. Then stood up and turned her back. "Unzip me. Please."

I was only too happy to oblige, but of course I had to ask, "Why the sudden change of subject?"

Facing me again, she wriggled free of the top and let the dress slip to the floor. There was as usual almost nothing else to take off. "You're very tired or you wouldn't be thinking such awful things. What you need is to come to bed. You'll feel much better in the morning."

CHAPTER 17

The sad-faced scholarly man who handles our printing—his hobby is Talmudic commercial law—once told me that only the heavy one-hundred-percent-rag paper called kidskin is considered fine enough for the personal correspondence of the president of the United States. So when I caught sight of the smallish ecru kidskin envelope in the next morning's mail, addressed in real ink, not ballpoint, my first thought was that the president had finally come around. No more would the Marine Band, playing transcriptions of hit tunes from *Show Boat, Oklahoma!*, and that all-time presidential favorite, *Fiddler on the Roof*, be the favored music at White House functions. At long last, they were ready for culture and us.

"It's not from the Oval Office," Jackie said. "It's from your girlfriend."

"The First Lady and I have never been close," I said.

"These scurrilous press stories are outrageous and without foundation."

"Try Sally Boyle."

"No kidding? What does she have to say?"

"Read it."

"'Dear Jackie and Alan,'" I read aloud, "'I am writing to ask if you and your friends in the Antiqua Players would play for us at the memorial service for dear Jerry at the Kennedy Center in Washington on Sunday, the fourth of May.' My God, that's three weeks from now."

"Never mind that. Go on."

"'Jerry loved your music, and so do we all, and nothing could be more comforting than to enjoy it yet again. . . .' She wants it brief, a half hour or so plus accompany a singer in one or two numbers. They're going to try to get Marianne Ramsay. They'll pay us. Full fee plus expenses, take it up with Ray Gerard. 'Please say yes, it would mean so much.' God, Jackie, I don't see how we can refuse."

"I don't either," Jackie said. "We'd better get hold of everybody and let them know. And I don't have a thing to wear."

"One good thing," I began.

"I know what you're going to say," Jackie said ruefully. "This solves the problem of what excuse do we use to talk to Gerard."

Not only did we not need an excuse, we didn't even need to make a phone call, because twenty minutes later Gerard himself called. He wanted to know if we'd heard from Mrs. Boyle, and if we had, whether the arrangements were satisfactory. I told him they were. I was wondering how to get him to see us in person when he solved that problem too.

"We're starting to go over Mr. Boyle's personal effects," he said. "For the estate. There's a whole collection of music. I was wondering whether you or maybe your harpsichord man—his name is Mitchell, right?—would want to help us sort through it, tell us what's involved, advise us on valuable items, things like that. We'd be happy to pay for your time."

I promised Gerard I'd check with Ralph and call him back and added that Jackie and I would both be happy to pitch in as well. He seemed pleased, but he wasn't half as pleased as I was. I explained to Jackie, and called Ralph. First I filled him in on Jackie's and my encounter with Kitty.

"Fascinating," he said. "And she thinks Gerard's the one?"

"She wants us to think so, anyway," I said. "But wait, there's more." I told him about Gerard's invitation.

"What fun! Let's do it!"

That was all I needed. I got back to Gerard and made an appointment for the next afternoon at three thirty.

Needless to say, it was raining when the cab let us out at Henderson Place. Except for a woman half hidden under her umbrella, who hailed our taxi and drove off, the little cobbled enclave was empty. When I pressed the bell at Boyle's front door, I expected to hear it echoing forlornly through a bare and deserted mansion out of a Gothic novel, but of course it didn't do any such thing. A moment later Gerard let us into the same warm bright interior I remembered from the night of the concert.

"We'll go right into the music room." He led us through the vast living room–library where we'd played and opened a door at the far end. "In here."

"Good gracious," said Ralph.

Jackie and I said nothing.

The room was roughly the same size as our studio, but there, believe me, all resemblance ceased. This room had a charcoal gray carpet; the walls were covered in a lighter gray fabric that looked like silk. It had the subdued feel of an exclusive art gallery. Discreet cove lighting supplied shadow-free illumination of just the right candlepower. A stylus recorded temperature and humidity levels on a rotating drum in a small glass-fronted climate control center. In a corner, a humidifier purred.

One whole wall was lined with shelves for records, tapes, and compact disks. Cabinetry for the multispeaker hi-fi system was built in; the speakers themselves were set into the walls. Two easy chairs were precisely placed to allow their occupants to enjoy the maximum stereo effect. Built-ins also lined the wall opposite the hi-fi. These, by their shallow drawers and brass label-holders, held music.

But it wasn't the sleek opulence of Boyle's inner sanctum that really took our breath away. It was the harpsichords.

There were four of them. The largest stood on a little dais of its own at the far end of the room. Two others were ranged along the wall that held the music cabinets. The fourth, off to one side, had a heavy quilted cloth cover strapped around it. By this and by its size, we recognized it. It was the instrument we'd used aboard *Enchantress*, the one Boyle had presumably been playing when he was killed. It was home now and back in place, but nobody had bothered to take off its coat. Laugh at me if you want, but seeing it like that made me feel sad.

"May I?" Ralph asked politely.

"That's what you're here for," said Gerard.

Ralph knows harpsichord building, restoration, and maintenance far better than most harpsichordists. He'd learned the trade the hard way. After buying a wonderful 1742 Jacob Kirckman for a song from a junk dealer in England, he'd apprenticed himself to one of the best makers in New York for a full year, just to learn how to make his find playable, and its figured walnut case beautiful, once again.

So now, when he dropped to all fours and crawled under the first of Boyle's harpsichords with a flashlight, Gerard's eyebrows went up, but Jackie and I knew Ralph knew what he was doing.

It took Ralph about fifteen minutes to finish his inspection. Of the four harpsichords on display, two, he said, seemed to be antiques dating from the early eighteenth century. If they could be authenticated, they'd be worth tens of thousands of dollars. Properly restored and made playable, they'd sell for even more. The other two were modern reproductions. The one from *Enchantress* was of good quality. The one on the dais, Boyle's favorite, was superb, as good as all but the finest restored period instruments.

Gerard was impressed. "Sounds like you know your onions. If we want to sell any of them, what do we do?"

I could almost see Ralph struggling with temptation. He already had two harpsichords. If he wanted that big one of Boyle's, he'd have to ask his trustees to invade capital, which he dislikes doing and the trustees loathe. Otherwise he'd have to make an offer for all four of the Boyle instruments, in the hope that he could unload three of them for enough money to pay for the one he wanted.

In the end, he decided not to go for it. With a sigh of regret, he gave Gerard the names of one or two dealers in keyboard instruments and a restorer. He also supplied the name of the woman at Sotheby's who was supposedly their house expert in the field.

Then we began opening drawers and going over Boyle's music. There was a ton of it, almost all for keyboard. It ranged from standard editions of the masters to privately printed volumes of works by composers so obscure that even Ralph had to shake his head in wonderment.

"Balbastre, okay," he said. "Him I know. He's not your Bach or Handel or even your Couperin, but people play him. In fact, he's kind of a fad right now. But Johann Krieger's double fugues, suites, and chaconnes? Give me a break!"

"What'll we do with it all?" asked Gerard.

"Good question," Ralph said. "Is anyone else in the family musical?"

"Beats me," Gerard said. "Maybe one of the nieces or nephews."

"What I'd do in that case is keep the standard stuff that they might want to play and sell off the rarities. Here, I'll give you a couple more names. What do you think, Alan, Haas in London?"

"Yeah, and what's-his-name at Blackwell's and Pendler on Sixth Avenue. They all buy printed music," I told Gerard, "and they're all okay."

"What about you people?" he asked.

"Keyboard music is Ralph's bag," I said.

"There are one or two items I'd love, I must admit," Ralph allowed. "But you're better off selling to a stranger."

Gerard looked amused. "Don't be too honest," he said. "This whole deal doesn't amount to more than maybe one percent of the estate. Tell you what, why don't you take your pick of any ten of these music books, and we'll call it your fee."

"God, how can I argue with that?"

"You can't," Jackie said. "Go ahead and pick."

"Five o'clock," Gerard said afterward. "You folks have time for a drink? Very nice. Right this way."

He sat us around the library fireplace—some invisible hand had already lighted a fire—and dispensed drinks from a tray-table set up as a bar.

I asked him if he'd heard from the police on Grand Turk.

"Nah, nothing. Not a blessed thing. And if you ask me, we're not likely to. They don't want any part of this mess."

He spoke with such finality that none of us felt like challenging him. But I decided that it was now or never with Gerard, so I plunged right in. "The other day Jackie ran into Kitty Feuerman. Kitty said something about getting together, but she didn't give Jackie her phone number. Do you by any chance have it?"

Gerard smiled. "Sure I do. But let me be honest. I really don't feel like giving it to you. Because frankly I think that woman is very, very bad news, and I don't care who knows it."

"What do you mean?" Jackie asked.

"Never mind. She'll take up your time and try to make you feel sorry for her and drive you crazy. So, no. If I were you, I'd forget about calling her. You'll be a lot better off."

"As a matter of fact," I said, "Mrs. Feuerman had some interesting things to say about you, too."

"I'll bet I know what they were," Gerard said. "She told you I murdered someone, right?"

"Her term for it was you shot him in cold blood," I said.

"God damn it," Gerard said without much heat, "she's been spreading that story for years. It's true I shot someone who got in the house here one night. I hit him in the shoulder and knocked him right down the stairs and it was a hell of a mess. But I slapped a tourniquet on him until the ambulance came and he was fine. Fine? The son of a bitch wanted to sue me for violating his civil rights. John Brendan Murphy, his name was. Needless to say, he didn't get anywhere with that."

"But he didn't die?" Jackie asked.

"Die? Brendan Murphy?" Gerard said. "Maybe he did. People do, you know, all the time. But it was ten years ago and I'll tell you this, he was okay when he showed up in court and they gave him two to five for breaking and entering. You can look up the whole record at Criminal Court, one hundred Centre Street. Just go to the docket room."

"Oh," Jackie said.

"What's Mrs. Feuerman's theory?" Gerard asked. "That if I shot John Brendan Murphy ten years ago I must have shot Mr. Boyle last week?"

"There were some other things," I said.

When I finished telling him what, he shrugged angrily. "What can I say? Mrs. Boyle feels bad about Mrs. Feuerman and so do I, I guess. But if she goes around saying crazy things like that, there's going to be trouble. I didn't shoot Mr. Boyle and I don't know who did. The woman is cuckoo, that's the only word for it. If I were you, I wouldn't have anything to do with her. I mean that."

I was all set to say I thought he was probably right when Gerard dropped his real bombshell. "Listen," he said, "if you have to poke around to find out who did it, why don't you talk to Mr. Boyle's other gal?"

"Other gal?" I parroted. "You mean Lauren Winship?"

"That's the one. I didn't want to tell anybody, but I'm not about to stick my head in that crazy woman's frame. Yeah, Lauren. She was on the boat the whole time."

CHAPTER 18

*W*hy did I do it? For a lark," Lauren Winship said. She smiled. Her fingers played with the gold chain at her throat. "It was a lark, too. It was amazing fun. Until . . ."

Through the floor-to-ceiling windows behind Lauren and David, Jackie and I had a breathtaking view of the West Side and the Hudson, backed up by a smoky mauve-and-purple sunset over New Jersey.

Here on the fortieth floor, the waiters and waitresses were young, brisk and attractive, most of them clearly budding stage talent. Up here, the clientele was young, noisy, and cheerful, Wall Streeters and midtowners warming up before dinner and a night in the clubs. There couldn't have been a more telling contrast than the one between Lauren's choice of restaurants and Kitty Feuerman's gloomy place of refuge.

"I have to admit it was exciting," Lauren was saying. "I was going to fly down anyway and meet the boat on Grand

Turk, but he called me. 'Why wait? Fly down to the Keys tomorrow and stow away. I'll tell Hayward you're coming. Bring your black lace and your lap-top,' that's what he said, 'this is a working holiday.' 'Which is the work part and which is the holiday?' I said, and he laughed. Well, God, how could anybody resist?"

If David was distressed by Lauren's confession, it didn't show. He was too busy signaling our waiter, who came bounding over with a sunny smile. "Could you please bring us some more cheese popcorn? Bring a big bowl this time, okay?"

Lauren gave him a look that said, Don't interrupt again, and went on to tell how, when she'd showed up at *Enchantress*'s berth—it was the day before we arrived—Hayward had duly installed her in the cabin adjoining Boyle's. And there, she declared, she'd spent most of the next couple of days.

"I sneaked out in the mornings early," she said, "to sunbathe and get some fresh air. And I want you to know that I heard your concert, too, and it was beautiful."

"Where were you, up on the top deck behind the funnel?" I asked.

"Right. How did you guess?"

"I came up there the second morning," I said, "and I knew I was smelling suntan lotion. But it never occurred to me to wonder whose it was."

"It was mine all right," Lauren said. She pushed the pasta around on her dinner plate, took a sip of wine and smiled again. She was utterly un-selfconscious about her stowaway caper. "What's to feel funny about?" she said. "I wasn't doing anything *wrong*. Oh, sure, there would have been a terrible scene if *she'd* caught me. *So* embarrassing. And I must say if I'd known his *mother* was going to be on board, I might never have done it. But none of that happened. And now it doesn't matter."

She made it all seem oddly vivid, the luxurious isolation, the hard work—she was racing to finish a cost-benefit analysis of the bank deal—the surreptitious visits from Boyle, the bouts of lovemaking. "Then, whoa! I was sound asleep in Jerry's bed when in walked Ray Gerard and switched on the light. He had a big bandage on his head and he looked awful. 'Wake up, we've got a problem,' he said. 'We've got to get you out of here.' 'Where's Jerry?' I said. 'He can't come, but he wants you to go. He sends love.'" This time Lauren's smile had pain in it. "He wasn't in any shape to do that, was he?"

"Not really," I said. "Not by then."

She went on to describe her getaway. "Ray had a little putt-putt alongside and I climbed down the ladder into the putt-putt and one of the crew handed down my bag and my computer and jumped in and took me ashore. He went back and a minute or two later *Enchantress* . . . took off."

"You must have been scared out of your wits," Jackie said.

"Not really. I couldn't imagine what Jerry was up to. But I knew he wasn't just going to abandon me. Someone would come."

Sure enough, someone had.

Gerard had had Captain Hayward radio a friend who had a cabin cruiser for charter. Within five minutes, the friend had picked Lauren off the beach and they were off to Cockburn Town. "I already had reservations at the Sea Salt, and you know the rest."

I finished the last shrimp on my plate. It was as disappointing as the seven others, but that was acceptable; it went with my mood. "So what you're saying is that even though you were right there, you have no idea at all who could have done the killing."

"I really don't. I mean, I knew there had been a huge fight with *her*, because he came in and told me all about it. But I just can't believe she killed him. And who else would want to? The rest of us were going to have some fun and maybe make a lot of money."

"What makes you think Kitty Feuerman didn't do it?" Jackie said.

"I don't know. I only met her once, so I don't know. But

I see her as the type who likes to make scenes, not kill someone."

Hmph. "Anybody want dessert?" I asked.

Jackie passed. I passed. David asked for Nesselrode pudding.

"I never eat dessert," said Lauren. Then she laughed. "That's funny. It reminds me of something Jerry said that night. I was in my room—cabin, whatever you call it—and he was having this meeting with Everett Feuerman right next door. It only lasted a few minutes and Jerry came in to be with me. And later he said, and that's what your mentioning dessert reminded me of, he said, 'I'll bet Everett ate a double dip of ice cream tonight. That's what he always does when he feels sorry for himself.'

" 'Now how on earth would you know that?' I asked him. He was sort of vague. 'Oh, it's just one of those things you know about your friends,' he said. But I knew how he knew. *She* told him, of course."

"I remember he did have a double scoop that night," I said, "so it looks as if Boyle was right."

"For whatever that's worth," Lauren said. "David, if you're finished?" She said thanks and good night and hurried him off to the theater. Jackie and I stayed for the magic of the view, which was only somewhat lessened by the black hole that drinks and dinner for four had burned in our bank account.

"At least we know why Kitty Feuerman is so sure Ray Gerard was faking being knocked out," I said over coffee.

"That's right. She must have seen him going into Boyle's stateroom."

"Or up to the bridge to get Hayward to radio."

"Mmm. But all of that was later, *after* Boyle was killed. He certainly could have been out cold before and during."

"As for Lauren—"

"Alan, do you think David's safe with her?"

"Sure. He's just a morsel on her plate. The minute

another big enchilada comes along, he will be a morsel in her past."

"You hope," Jackie said.

"What did she take you to?" Jackie asked David the next afternoon.

"I dunno. Some weird thing. Three people sitting around a table talking about how bad things are, they wish they could be turned into butterflies."

"Butterflies?"

"Yeah. Then they could go floating across the fields contributing to the great dance of nature."

"That sounds rich with meaning."

"Hey, look, it won an award."

"Come on," I said. "This is supposed to be a rehearsal."

David played a lazy little jazz riff on his lute. "Take it easy, babe. We don't even have to *look* at this material until July. You're dissipating your vital energy."

I looked at my watch. One minute past three. "Never mind about my vital energy, what about everybody else? Why can't we ever begin on time?"

"We *are* on time," said Terry, dropping his damp raincoat on the couch. He must have sneaked in when I wasn't looking. "Let's go."

"One thing before we start," said Ralph, trailing Terry by one step. "I've got to be out of here by five sharp. We've corralled all our soloists, even Ann-Marie, for a six-thirty run-through at the church. Ann-Marie can't stay past seven, because—"

"I don't give a goddamn about Ann-Marie and her scheduling problems," I exploded.

Ralph smiled gently and applied the needle. "Alan, it's not *our* fault that Jeremiah Boyle got himself shot."

I glared at him.

"I'll go make coffee," Terry said.

"Good idea," said Jackie. "He'll want it when he gets back from therapy."

In spite of myself, I started to laugh. "Okay, I apologize. I'm sorry I said what I said about Ann-Marie. She's a very nice human being for a soprano and has been known to sing up to tempo and on key for several minutes at a clip, unbelievable as this may sound. Now can we start rehearsal?"

We could, and to my surprise it went quite well and we were actually finished by five o'clock.

"Ralph . . ." I pointed to a stack of music books on the coffee table. The books were the ones he'd chosen at Boyle's two days before and dumped at our place. If I didn't say something, they'd soon be a permanent part of our scenery.

It was Ralph's turn to look at his watch. "Can't they wait?" he said. "They're heavy and I'm late and it's rush hour."

"Why don't you take them a couple at a time?" Jackie said tactfully.

"Oh, all right." He scooped up several, including one with a navy cover. If he hadn't been in a hurry, it would never have slipped out from under his arm and dropped to the floor.

I stooped to pick it up. "Hey. Isn't this . . . ?"

"Yes," Ralph said impatiently. "It's the Jacobi Rameau. My copy's in absolute tatters, and this one's almost brand new. Now—"

"It's what Boyle was playing from when he was killed. Gerard must have grabbed it and brought it back with the rest of Boyle's stuff. You've got a real collector's item." I leafed through it curiously.

"Alan, please. I'm in a *hurry*."

"Wait just a second," I said. "This is interesting."

A page from a small notebook had been folded in half and stuck in the Jacobi as a bookmark. I could see that there was handwriting on the page.

"Hey," Terry intoned in a haunted-house voice. "A message from beyond the grave."

I unfolded the paper. On it was a note in tiny neat script.

"'Shaver,'" I read aloud, and then underneath it, "'give him one hundred.' God knows what that means. Does anybody at least know Boyle's handwriting?"

Nobody did, so I made a phone call and spoke to Ray Gerard.

"Sure," he said. "He was always writing himself notes. On a little pad he carried around. Is the writing real small? That's him, all right. What does it say?"

I read it to him.

"Well, that's Shaver the lawyer, of course. But I haven't any idea what it means. Sounds a little like Mr. Boyle was awarding him a perfect score on something. But who knows?"

I thanked him and rang off.

"Okay, so he wrote it, so what?" Terry said.

"I don't know," I said. "But it's got something to do with the bank deal. I'll bet money on it."

"Don't bet too much," said Ralph over his shoulder. "It could be some other deal involving Shaver. It could be two separate notes, one to remind him to talk to Shaver, one about something completely different. I'm going now. Good-bye, everybody." He fled.

"That so-and-so," I said, remembering Shaver. "He'll never tell us anything."

"If there's anything to tell," Jackie said.

CHAPTER 19

_W_e know too much," I complained to Jackie the next morning.

It was true.

In music, you have to be able to think about lots of different things at once. But just taking the inventory of what we'd found out about Boyle's murder was overloading my circuits. Kitty fingering Gerard. Gerard up and around when everybody thought he was immobilized. Lauren present the whole time, an economist playing the lead in a bedroom farce with a tragic ending. Feuerman eating too much ice cream. Boyle giving Shaver a hundred of something before he died. I shook my head dispiritedly and poured more coffee. "Everybody's got something incriminating to say about everybody else, but nothing fits, nothing adds up."

"In that case, maybe you should stop worrying about it," Jackie said.

"You're not being helpful," I said. In a different voice I added, "In fact, you're being quite distracting."

"Ouch," Jackie said a second later. "If the Great Detective is absolutely determined to eat my ear for breakfast instead of his English muffin, the least he could do is shave."

"The Great Detective is going to have to stop detecting for a while," I said. "I have to practice. The tuner's coming to do the little harpsichord. And I've got Vikki at four."

"So you do, you poor thing," Jackie said.

Vikki is the bratty twelve-year-old—twelve going on forty—whose musical education is the blight of my Tuesdays. I'd already delivered Vikki's expensive new violin. Now I was going to have to give her a lesson on it. Vikki's mother, divorced and breathing vengeance against maledom, believes with eye-bulging intensity that her daughter is the next Salerno-Sonnenberg. This means that Vikki is encouraged to grow a lot of hair, not comb it, and be obnoxious. I have frequently threatened to throttle Vikki, but unfortunately the child does have talent; and not only that, her father, who pays for the lessons, is the reigning King of Orthodontia in southern Westchester and hence a highly reliable source of income.

At five o'clock, having survived Vikki, I strolled uptown. Jackie and I were to meet at Seventy-fifth and Central Park West, where she was giving her last lesson of the day. It was still light out, one of those blue-gray early spring evenings in New York that make you forget the freezing miseries past and blithely dismiss the steamy awfulness ahead.

"Safe home," the doorman called as we left.

We would have made it all the way, but fate, urban topography, and the demands of commerce decided otherwise.

You need to know that the usual gloomy cement walkway separates our building from the building next door. It slopes down from street level and leads to the small paved courtyard behind our building and to the rear entrance. The walkway is wide enough for movers and tradespeople to go in and out. Only the occasional dummy does this, of course. Why bother? It's so much simpler to pay the modest toll exacted by Ramón and his associates, trundle the load through the lobby, and use the passenger elevator.

New York being New York, our walkway is guarded by a formidable-looking wrought-iron gate. Above the gate is a cheveaux-de-frise arrangement of sharp curly spikes that would do credit to Alcatraz in the glory days, and in recent years this has been augmented by a generous topping of razor-edged concertina wire. I kid you not: the place is impregnable. Or rather, it would be impregnable except for one minor flaw. The gate is seldom locked during the day and is never locked at night.

I asked Ramón about this once—not complaining, you understand, just curious—and he looked at me pityingly. "I lock the gate, how we're gonna get our deliveries?"

"Don't they go through the lobby, like always?"

"'Ey, no, man! *Our* deliveries."

Then I caught on. The car thieves who supply Ramón's growing autoparts enterprise are people who prefer not to advertise their presence. The alleyway is their route of choice, and blocking so vital an artery of trade is contrary to Ramón's extreme laissez-faire economic philosophy. "I mean, man, how we gonna make our livin', you do that?"

Which explains how on a pleasant evening, with plenty of pedestrian traffic in the streets, an assailant could slip into a shadowy nook no more than forty feet from our well-lit front door and keep watch unseen, or at least unremarked, until Jackie and I came within range.

I don't think I ever heard the footsteps.

The first thing I felt was a blow, more like a hard shove, that caught me in the small of the back and sent me reeling. I know I yelled something. That's when a second shove, a really brutal one, knocked me off my feet and halfway into the gutter between two parked cars.

I was struggling to get up when I heard Jackie scream.

I spun around to see her sitting on the sidewalk, her skirt up over her knees. She was clutching her right side in the region of her waist. Her face was tense with shock and pain.

I also saw our attacker. A dim figure in a dark flapping coat, he, or maybe she, was running furiously across Amsterdam Avenue against the light and in the teeth of heavy northbound traffic. I remember thinking viciously, Get mashed by a bus, you bastard. But I had no hope of catching whoever it was, and no time to waste on pursuit.

"It hurts," Jackie whimpered like a child.

"Let's see." I dropped to my battered knees by her side. To my horror. I saw blood trickling through her fingers. I didn't know what to do.

People on the sidewalk edged away and walked faster when they saw us. "Watch out, she's drunk," I overheard one of them say. Fuck you too, buddy.

"What happen?" Incarnación, looking worried, came up to us.

"You better dial nine-one-one," I said. "Tell them it's a stabbing."

"First I go get Dr. Barnhard."

"What good will he do? He's a shrink."

Incarnación ignored me. Much later, I realized how dumb my request was. Asking Incarnación to call the cops was like asking Ronald Reagan to raise taxes. "The doctor gotta late patient tonight, I go get him." He trotted off.

I'll say this for Dr. Barnhard, he came running. And ruining the crease on his trousers and getting street dirt and blood all over them didn't seem to perturb him at all.

"If you could just move your hand and lean back a little," he said calmly to Jackie. "That's it." He rolled her sweater clear of the damage.

I watched in astonishment as he tore the wrapper off a square of sterile gauze. How come a psychiatrist had ordinary first-aid stuff on hand?

Dr. Barnhard must have been reading my thoughts. "Don't worry," he said, "I used to be a real doctor once." He mopped away blood. "Now. Let's have a look. Mmm . . . nasty but superficial. Right along the rib. I doubt if you'll even need stitches. If you could hold the pad against it. Yes, like that. Now, any other wounds?"

Jackie shook her head.

He looked at me questioningly.

"No problem except being shook up," I said.

"Do you think you can walk?" he asked Jackie. "If you can make it as far as my office, I'll fix up that cut."

"I can walk," Jackie said. "I think I'm more scared than anything else."

"You and me both," I said.

The doctor and I helped Jackie to her feet. As she stood up, something little and shiny fell out of her lap and dropped with a tinkle on the sidewalk. I bent to pick it up.

"Be careful," Dr. Barnhard said.

In the best detective-story tradition, I used my handkerchief to avoid smudging any fingerprints.

"Aha." The doctor smiled, "The murder weapon."

It was a small delicate pair of scissors. Its silvery blades were curved at the points, its handles were gold.

"Maybe from a sewing box," I said.

"If we could please continue this investigation in my office," Dr. Barnhard said, urging us slowly in that direction.

"Who the hell could it have been?" I asked Jackie, but she just shook her head. I wasn't surprised. Her assailant had taken pains not to be recognized.

Instead of alcohol and disinfectant, Dr. Barnhard's office smelled of cigar smoke and sweat, which I took to be the clinical odor of psychiatry. But in the inner cubbyhole along with his desk was a wall cabinet well stocked with conventional medical supplies.

"This will sting, but not unbearably." Within minutes, the doctor had cleaned and bandaged the three-inch cut on Jackie's side. He'd even asked her whether she was allergic to surgical tape. "There's no mad hurry," he said, "but you ought to show that to your own doctor. And when you get home, I'd suggest a cup of hot sweet tea and take it easy for an hour or two. Maybe you can figure out what kind of scissors these are.

"I'm not going to give you any nonsense about your emotional reactions. You'll have them, of course, but you look like healthy people who can handle them. Talk to each other. Be open. That's about all anybody can say. Except that you must of course report this to the police."

"What good will that do?" I said. "The person who did it is long gone. The police won't even bother to investigate."

Dr. Barnhard said mildly, "That may be. But it's your duty. Besides, the officers tell me that they base their manpower decisions on statistics. So if you report it, perhaps they will give us more police."

"We'll tell the police," Jackie promised.

"I can't thank you enough," I said from the heart. "How much do we owe you?"

Dr. Barnhard looked shocked. "Owe me? For helping somebody hurt in the street? Nothing, that's what. Boy, some nerve you've got, insulting me like that!" His mock-angry expression turned into a smile. "You'd better scoot out of here before I lose my temper."

Decency. It happens. Even in New York. "Doctor, do you by any chance like music?"

"Music? I love music. Why do you ask? Don't tell me, I already know. You're some of those musicians from upstairs, am I right?"

It turned out that the doctor had all the old Noah Greenberg New York Pro Musica thirty-threes in his collection and listened to them over and over.

"We're playing at Alice Tully Hall on October thirteenth," I said, "and two orchestra seat tickets will be in the mail to you as soon as they're printed."

"That's extraordinarily kind of you. Take care of that cut. Please, I must go. If there's one thing my wife hates, it's to have her pot roast dry out."

We said good-bye and took ourselves up in the elevator.

I called around to let the others know what had happened. Then we called the police. They wanted us both to come right down in person, but Jackie was too exhausted and upset, so I left her lying on the sofa in the studio and walked over to the Twentieth Precinct. The woman on the desk took down my story politely, expressed her sympathy and wished us a better evening from then on, but it was clear from the word *go* that the Twentieth Precinct had more urgent concerns that night than ourselves.

I picked up a big container of chicken soup on the way home, and a couple of corned beef sandwiches on rye. "Salt and fluids, that's what you need when you've lost blood," I said to Jackie.

"Oh, thank you, doctor," she said. She drank the soup, ate two bites of her sandwich, and fell asleep on the sofa.

I lowered my magazine and watched and listened while her breathing evened out and her muscles relaxed. And sitting there in the tranquil studio, I began to shake with anger.

Somebody had hurt Jackie.

Why?

Either to scare her or silence her, which was the same thing, really. Or, which was still the same thing, to threaten her as a way to make us stop asking questions about Boyle's murder.

I cursed rich, arrogant Jeremiah Boyle for getting himself murdered.

I cursed Chief Inspector Nye for caving in to the realities of his job and thereby exposing Jackie to hurt.

On an unrelated subject, I cursed all of Boyle's friends for their unrestrained greed.

But most of all, I cursed myself.

I was responsible for Jackie. Not that she'd thank me for saying so, you understand, but damn it, in some primitive corner of my male psyche there lurked the certainty that I *was*. And I'd done nothing to protect her.

That had to change. To make it change, there were two things I had to do.

"Ralph, we need Henry," I said softly into the receiver.

"Henry, right. I'll get his number and call you back."

A year or so ago, a friend of Ralph's broke up with his lover. As Ralph explained delicately, "There were problems. My friend hired Henry for a week. No more problems." Ralph mentioned that Henry was from uptown. That meant he was black.

"Why weren't there any more problems?" I asked.

"If you saw Henry, you'd understand why."

"You want to scare someone," said Henry on the phone. "We don't do that sort of work."

"No, no, I want to scare someone *off*," I explained.

"That's different," Henry said. "I imagine we can do that. Starting when and for how long?"

"How about now?"

"It's only for a few days," I said to Jackie. "The idea is that whoever is after you will see that someone is guarding you and will get nervous and go away."

She wanted to know how much Henry would charge.

I told her and she winced.

It was going to cost us a hundred dollars a day plus lunches for about four hours of "exterior protective service." But for once she didn't protest. At least, not very much. A three-inch slash along the ribs is a powerful argument in favor of protection. And that was before I introduced the two of them to each other. I did that at ten o'clock the next morning.

"Can I call you Jackie?" said Henry, in a dark gray flannel suit, blue and white striped shirt, and foulard tie.

"Of course," Jackie said.

He nodded at her gamba. "Is that thing heavy? I assume you carry it around."

"It's not too bad," she told him. "Why?"

"I wouldn't want you to think I was rude not to carry it," Henry explained. "You need a porter, we'll get you a porter. But I'm your bodyguard. Means I have to have both hands, both eyes, both ears, all of me on the job all the time."

All of Henry was quite a lot. He stood six feet six. I would not describe him as willowy.

"I understand," Jackie said.

"Okay, now where are we going today?"

Feeling a lot happier, I left them to their scheduling and went to the second thing on my agenda.

Jackie looked in before she and Henry departed. "Alan, thank you. Henry and I are soul mates. Wait, though. How come you're putting on a suit?"

"I've got a date. On Wall Street. And it's a jungle down there."

Forrester, Fensterwald, Craig, Bellamy, and O'Rourke were the name partners. One of them had been a governor and one a secretary of state. All had long ago joined the great Bar Association in the sky, but their firm lived on here below. Lived on and prospered mightily, and Hugh Jackson Shaver with them.

An owlish young man in horn-rims came out to the reception area and led me up two flights of carpeted stairs. The seat of the young man's slacks was shiny and his shoes needed reheeling. I felt sorry for him until I reflected that he was probably already making five times as much as I made, and he was still only an associate, with partnership years away.

The young man ushered me into the library and left me there. I wasn't invited to sit down so I went over to the windows. The view made the view from the restaurant the other night look like the inside of a sewer.

"French. Alan French the musician. You called, right? What was it you wanted?"

I turned.

Shaver was in shirt sleeves. His shirt was a blue button-down. His tie was yellow with little amoebas on it. At the sight of him, I could feel my blood pressure rise.

"That's right," I said. "I wonder if you could help me. It's about something that happened aboard *Enchantress*, in connection with the Swain's Bank takeover. And of course Jeremiah Boyle's murder."

Shaver's mouth hardened. "Nobody's proved it was murder. And everything I did in regard to that situation is either my own work product or is protected by attorney-client privilege. I don't know who you think you are, French, or what it is you want, but I don't see that I have to tell you one goddamn thing."

I made one last effort to be civil. "If I ask you a question, will you at least consider answering it?"

"I doubt it," he said disdainfully. "What's the question?"

The anger simmering in me finally boiled over. I walked slowly over to him, raised a finger and poked him right in his yellow necktie. "Listen, you dumb shit. My wife was stabbed last night. I don't know who did it, but it was no mugger, it was somebody connected with Boyle. You can help me find out who, and until you do I'm holding you responsible, *personally*, for what happened. Now, is that clear?"

Something in my face must have convinced him I was serious, because he blinked and nodded. "Oh. Well. What's your question?"

My question. I'd been framing it since the night before, going over and over everything we'd been told and everything we knew, focusing finally on Boyle's cryptic little message. Now I asked it.

And I got my answer.

CHAPTER 20

$\mathcal{T}$he travel cover of a harpsichord is custom made of heavy padded canvas duck, takes eight weeks to finish, is useless for any other purpose, and costs four hundred dollars.

Who in his right mind would steal one?

We have no idea, but bitter experience on tour has taught us that people will steal anything. So as soon as we positioned Ralph's second-biggest harpsichord on the Terrace Theater stage, Ralph folded the cover, took it to the house manager's office, and stood by while an assistant house manager locked it in a closet. Only then did he go back to our dressing room, turn green, and give way to his usual preconcert misery.

Fortunately, the Kennedy Center people understand these things.

The center, of course, is immense, vast enough to contain a full-scale opera house, an even larger concert hall, and three other performance spaces. The Terrace Theater, on the upper-most level, is the smallest of the five, and it can accommodate five hundred.

Our first look at its rose and silver decor came as something of a shock.

"Thank you, God," Jackie said with feeling.

"What for?" asked Terry.

"For making me pack a plain navy dress, that's what for."

Jackie, Terry, and I dressed quickly, wished Ralph well, left David to keep an eye on him, and went out front.

Sally Boyle wanted appropriate music while people were coming in. We'd decided on a subdued William Byrd viol fantasia. And we'd arranged not to be up on stage.

"If they see you there," the house manager had said shrewdly, "they'll think they're late and interrupting, so they'll stop and mill about and make noise and waste time." Instead, he'd put us at the front of the house on the left, near the stage but on a level with the first rows of seats.

We ended the fantasia and, according to plan, immediately began it again. We'd keep repeating it until all but the last few stragglers had negotiated the steps and found seats.

I glanced up from my music and saw that the ushers were closing the doors.

It looked as if at least several hundred invitees had showed up. I wagged a finger as we neared the end of the second run-through to signal that we'd only have to repeat the Byrd one more time.

Afterward, while the audience shed its furs, settled in its seats and rustled its programs—Sally Boyle had insisted on printed programs—we made our way through the door just behind us, climbed a few steps, and took our places in front of the beige acoustic shell they set up for music and roll away when they need the full stage for drama.

An ancient in a dark suit and a navy tie with white polka dots propped himself upright on a lectern and in a halting voice read a long, obscure poem.

Maybe I'm mistaken—Jackie and the others swear I'm not only mistaken but out of my mind—but I still think I heard the illustrious old bard compare Jeremiah Boyle, at various points in his composition, to Daniel Webster, to a wild turkey cock in full plumage, to Saint Sebastian the martyr, and to a box of Wheaties, Breakfast of Champions.

In the fullness of time, the poet, his head protruding tortoise-like from a collar grown too large, made an end and limped slowly away, accompanied by murmurs of admiration from the audience.

That made it Marianne's turn.

Few singers live up to their publicity. But Marianne Ramsay and her contralto are one great exception. If you've seen Ramsay on television, you know she's no imposing Brunhilde. She herself says, laughing, "I may not be tall, but God Almighty knows I'm not beautiful." But when she sings, she *is* beautiful. Her face lights up, her squat pudgy body moves, her hands move too, her mouth opens wide and that big, big voice of hers comes pouring out. I could listen to her all day long, doing never mind what—lieder, cantatas, spirituals, opera, you name it.

Ramsay walked out on stage this evening in a simple dark green street dress, carrying her music in one hand. She certainly didn't go with the decor, but who cared? She planted herself in the curve of the harpsichord and paused, a thoughtful expression on her brown face. She gave an almost imperceptible nod and Ralph and Jackie slid into the striding three-bar bass theme that opens and underlies all of her first song, one of the loveliest ever written.

"Music . . ." Ramsay sang softly,

"Music . . . for a while
Shall all your cares beguile . . ."

It was a wonderful choice for a memorial service, Henry Purcell's song about the healing powers of music. I've heard it a hundred times, but listening to it this time I had to blink back tears. Not God knows on account of Jeremiah Boyle, but because Ramsay had me believing that this craft of ours really can, for a while, make the snakes of anger and vengeance drop bewitched from Alecto's head.

From the stage, I could easily see Sally Boyle. She was seated on the left aisle about halfway up the house. She seemed perfectly self-possessed, but I noticed she was holding a handkerchief in one hand. I wondered how she was responding to the music and beamed her a silent message of good will.

I picked out other familiar faces scattered all through the deeply raked house: the Sensabaughs; Williamson and Mrs. Williamson; Shaver; Henry, huge and reassuringly solid in the first row. The Feuermans? I thought I had Everett spotted, but it turned out to be someone else, someone I'd never seen before. And just when I started to look for Kitty Feuerman, it was time to pick up my treble viol and go back to work.

Ramsay's second song, Byrd's "Ye Sacred Muses" for voice and viols, would have been better at the end of the program, but Ramsay had to catch a plane for the West Coast and couldn't wait around, so we had to do it then and there. She sang it beautifully, but whenever I think of that evening, her Purcell is what I remember.

After Ramsay went off, David and Terry played a lute and tenor viol arrangement of John Dowland's "Captain Digorie Piper His Galliard." We'd chosen the Dowland for its haunting, elegiac quality. We certainly hadn't told our Boyle sponsors who Digorie Piper was: a Cornish adventurer in Elizabethan times who'd narrowly escaped hanging for piracy. But to us, he did seem to have a lot in common with Jeremiah Boyle.

Next, a second gentleman, much younger than the poet but according to the program no less eminent, took to the podium and read a brief account of life at prep school with Jeremiah Boyle. He had amusing tales to tell, and he told them amusingly. They drew chuckles from the audience, and once or twice Sally Boyle's face relaxed into a pleased, reminiscent smile. Yet the man left me with the feeling that, in actual fact, being Jeremiah Boyle's prep school roommate hadn't been much fun at all.

Of course, by the time he was nearing the end of his talk I was thinking of something quite different. Namely, the first note of the Bach Sonata in F Minor for Violin and Harpsichord, BWV 1018.

Why, I asked myself, why of all the violin pieces in the repertoire, did you have to pick this one?

Because it's so gorgeous, dummy, myself answered. And you know perfectly well that if you can get by the first note, you can play the whole rest of the piece.

Even the double-stops in the third movement?

Even the double-stops. So pick up your violin now, while Mr. Prep School is winding down, and get ready to play.

But the first note . . .

Let me explain why it's such a bastard. The F Minor opens, slowly and calmly, with five full bars for harpsichord, and gamba. Midway through the sixth bar, the violin part begins with a long, long held note, a middle C, to be exact. This had to be quiet. It has to be even: no lurching or swelling or cornball heavy vibrato. And it has to lead naturally into the violin's first musical utterance.

See what I mean?

Whenever I contemplate the F Minor, I think of a painter standing, brush in hand, before a huge blank canvas. He knows he has to give it one clean stroke to start. If he gets it right, he'll paint a masterpiece. If he gets it wrong, his career is shattered.

The sweat began to collect around my hairline.

Mr. Prep School gathered up his papers and left the stage. I stood up. I didn't want to stand up. I wanted to go back to the dressing room. They have wonderful dressing rooms at the Kennedy Center. They even have showers, and the hot water is hot. Wouldn't it be a good idea to take a relaxing hot shower? I could play much better after a shower.

"Let's tune," I croaked to the others. We tuned.

It was Jackie's turn to worry about my state of mind. "Are you okay?"

"No," I whispered.

"Don't worry," my unfeeling spouse whispered back, "you'll be much better once we've started."

Thanks, Jackie.

Ralph did one of his patented eyebrow tricks to give us the beat and he and Jackie, as one, embarked on BWV 1018.

They'd gotten as far as the start of measure three when I, staring numbly out at the audience, suddenly crossed gazes with Everett Feuerman. He must have come late and slipped in while we were tuning. He was sitting right next to Sally Boyle. It made every kind of sense for him to show up, but seeing him there jarred my already jangled nerves.

Measure four. Not that it mattered, but why was the man watching us so intently, like a scientist examining a new kind of bug?

Measure five. Time to concentrate. Yes, but—

Measure six. Almost by reflex, my mind on Feuerman, my arm and wrist moved the bow slowly across that middle C. With mild surprise, I listened to the note that came out. It was gentle but rock steady: I couldn't have played it better if I'd planned it that way.

Unperturbed by me and my violin, Ralph and Jackie continued their serene pursuit of their own musical business. I had another five-bar rest, and while I was waiting and listening, something about the music, something it was saying, nibbled at the edge of my consciousness.

What?

I don't know, and shut up because you're about to start in again and this time you keep going.

It's important.

The music is what's important. Ralph and Jackie are doing wonderfully. Your own theme is hidden in what they're playing. It's time to bring it into the open.

Understanding coursed through me like an electric current. *The hidden theme*. It had to be.

For Christ's sake, play, will you?

For the second time, I launched into that long middle C. Only this time, instead of finishing it off with a shy little cadence I kept on going into the violin's main musical statement, playing freely, plunging into the music because the music was confirming what I'd begun working out the night Jackie was attacked, outside our apartment, what I'd known for certain since my stormy little interview with Hugh Shaver. Namely, that Everett Feuerman, and not Kitty Feuerman or Ray Gerard or anybody else, had murdered Jeremiah Ten Brinck Gardner Boyle.

CHAPTER   21

don't want your congratulations, you bloody-minded bastard," I said.

He didn't even blink.

"You see, I've figured it out. I've figured out the one thing that makes sense of all the rest."

"How impressive," Feuerman said coldly.

Jackie was at my left, Ralph at my right. Terry and David were acting as flankers. Feuerman stood before us like a conductor, but we were done with music for that day.

It was a queer place for a confrontation, the open-air terrace of the Kennedy Center on a balmy spring evening. The lights of the city were on display. Waiters were moving quietly to and fro. On all sides, civilized people were exchanging pleasant platitudes and paying us no attention whatever. A blasted heath would have been more appropriate, or a craggy mountainside. Or an empty, echoing room in Boyle's deserted house in New York, with the rain splashing down outside.

But it didn't matter. I was conscious of an overpowering weary anger that this business had gone on so long. It had to be finished, and finished tonight.

"Why don't you stop me?" I taunted him. "Why don't you tell Mrs. Boyle to have the guards throw me out?"

"There is no need to bother Sally Boyle," he said. "You are overwrought from playing—even if you won't accept my congratulations, I will still say you were quite brilliant—and from the memorial. It's understandable. These affairs are always unsettling."

"Well, then, why don't you turn your back and walk away?"

He shrugged. "Maybe I am curious."

"Fine," I said. "I'll do my best to satisfy your curiosity."

"No doubt, Mr. Holmes, your deductions will be more logical if I offer you a glass of wine," Feuerman said, "or perhaps some cocaine."

I brushed aside the heavy-handed sarcasm. "All along, the one thing you've been able to hide behind is lack of motive. You seem to have had no reason in the world to want Jeremiah Boyle dead—and every reason to want him to live."

"Naturally I did. He was my close friend."

"It's true your wife was Boyle's mistress," I said.

"So was yours," Feuerman said spitefully.

Jackie and I both laughed. That unforced laughter, I think, was the first dart to find its way through Feuerman's armor.

"Never," I said. "Boyle tried, all right, but he didn't know Jackie very well, and you don't, either. But that's beside the point. Your wife *was* Boyle's mistress. The thing was, everybody knew and nobody minded, including you."

"Correct," said Feuerman.

"It's also true that you're a very good shot with a rifle."

"Rifles aren't handguns," he said.

"Exactly," I said. "And even if you're terrific with a

pistol as well, several other people on that yacht were expert too. Furthermore, you were one of Jerry Boyle's key people in a very lucrative business deal. Anything that happened to Boyle might blow the whole deal apart and cost you a lot of money."

"For a person hired to entertain Jerry's guests, you seem to have amassed a great deal of private information," Feuerman said acidly.

"Oh, dear, one can't keep *anything* from the servants nowadays," I said. "But that was all to the good, wasn't it? The servants thought along with the cops and everybody else that you had a cast iron reason to *not* kill Jerry Boyle. Hell, you wouldn't even want him exposed to the common cold."

"That would appear obvious."

"But," I said, "what if something had gone really wrong?"

"What are you talking about?"

I paused. This was it. "What if you and Boyle had had a last-minute quarrel? What if he'd told you he was killing the Swain's Bank takeover?"

Feuerman looked at me as if I were something that had stuck to the sole of his shoe.

I pursued the point. "He'd done that before, hadn't he? In fact, that very morning he'd threatened to have Shaver call the whole thing off."

"How the devil did you find that out?" Feuerman said incredulously.

"Never mind," I said, "it's true. And that's just what did happen. You met with Boyle and he told you the takeover was off. *But you knew that nobody else knew.* So you went back later that night and shot him. You killed your friend to protect your stake in his deal."

"You're stark raving mad," he said.

"It's amazing," Jackie broke in. "You had the meeting and then you came back to the dinner table and ate a double helping of ice cream."

"You're both lunatics. I don't have to listen to any more of this!" But he made no move to break away.

A new thought struck me. "Could there have been a witness to that meeting?" I wondered out loud. "Could your wife have been in the room at the time?"

Feuerman's eyes were stony. His mouth stayed tight shut.

"Never mind," I said. "Whether she was there or not, Mrs. Feuerman had plenty of reason to be furious at Boyle. He was ignoring her and openly chasing Jackie. When she tried to hit back at him, he humiliated her in front of his guests. He'd even arranged to have Lauren Winship stow away aboard *Enchantress* to work on the bank deal and amuse him in her spare time."

"Impossible," Feuerman said thickly.

"Fact," I said.

It gave him pause. "Kitty wasn't jealous," he said finally. "Not any more than I was."

"So you say now. But what was in your mind when you went into the salon that night, walked over to Boyle as he was playing Rameau, and shot him with the gun from his bedside table, the gun Kitty Feuerman knew was there?"

"Sally! For God's sake, do you know what this madman is saying?"

I was focusing so hard on Feuerman that I hadn't seen Sally Boyle coming. Ray Gerard was at her side. She took one look at us and the polite smile on her face melted away. In its place came an expression I couldn't fathom. "No, Everett," she said, "what is the madman saying?"

"He's accusing me of murdering Jerry."

Gerard said and did nothing.

Sally's face turned gray and old before our eyes. But all she had to say was, "Really? How extraordinary. Alan, please go on."

I tried to keep my voice as matter-of-fact as hers. "I'm not sure there's much more to say. I was just telling Mr. Feuerman here that I'd figured things out. He had a fight with your son. Over money. So he killed him. And he's been trying to put the blame on his wife."

"Dear Alan, you can't believe that!" But her eyes told me that she knew I could.

"Sounds ridiculous, doesn't it? But look at him. He knows I'm right. He's scared we have proof. Otherwise, why would he be trying to kill my wife?"

I held my breath.

For a long, long moment, the two of them stared at each other.

"You lied to me, Everett," Sally said in her clear voice.

"Never, never did I try to kill her!" Feuerman exclaimed, his face working. "He's the one who lies! To frighten her, maybe, something like that . . ." His voice trailed off.

"Why ever would you want to frighten her, Everett?" Sally asked softly.

I answered for him. "Jackie was on deck that night. She went up to look at the stars. He saw her there on his way back from . . . doing what he'd done. And he thinks she might have seen him. That's why. He wanted to scare her into keeping quiet. At least that's what he wanted the first time. He faked a call from the police to lure her out and dropped a roofing tile in her path."

"What do you mean, 'the first time'?" Sally asked me.

"He did it again. The second time was back in New York. An odd thing happened. Kitty Feuerman bumped into Jackie accidentally on purpose, and then we all had a drink together. And Feuerman found out. I don't know whether he thought Jackie might have told Kitty something disastrous or whether Kitty might have told us something. But I do know what happened."

I told her briefly about the slashing. "And I'll bet there's a pair of little curved scissors missing from Kitty's manicure set, isn't there?"

But Feuerman had recovered his glacial composure. "You can prove nothing," he said.

I waited for him to go on, but that was all he said. The silence lengthened and lengthened. For the first time, I noticed that except for ourselves and a few waiters clearing away, the whole huge terrace was empty. Boyle's final well-wishers had departed.

"You swore to me it was Kitty," Sally Boyle said.

Nobody spoke.

"You came to my cabin that night," Sally said. "You told me that a dreadful, dreadful thing had happened. It was Kitty. She'd quarreled with Jerry and she'd been drinking and she'd taken his little gun from the bedside table and shot him with it. You begged me. There would be a scandal, you said. Jerry would be disgraced. Kitty would go to prison. Lives would be ruined. You pleaded. For Jerry's sake, for the family, for Kitty, we should all keep quiet. If we did, any investigation would soon peter out for lack of evidence. Those were your exact words.

"You said that putting poor Kitty on trial for murder would be senseless. It wouldn't bring Jerry back. It wouldn't make her suffer more than she was already suffering. You promised you'd take care of Kitty yourself. You'd arrange things so she couldn't harm anybody else ever again. Of course I agreed. I didn't think twice. And now it turns out that it was you all along."

"No, no, of course it wasn't," said Feuerman.

"That you killed Jerry over money."

"It was Kitty!"

Ray Gerard cleared his throat. "You're saying Mrs. Feuerman knew just how to put me to sleep? Interesting. Where'd she learn that?"

"Was it Kitty who tried to stab my wife?" I demanded. "Why would she do that, if she already knew you knew?"

Our questions hung in the air.

"For God's sake!" Feuerman shouted, so loudly that one of the waiters looked curiously in our direction. "There isn't a shred of proof of any of this craziness!"

"But it *is* true," Sally said, tilting her head back to look him in the face. "Isn't it?"

"I deny it absolutely," mumbled Feuerman, not meeting her gaze.

We all stood rooted to the pavement. No wonder: there's not a syllable in Emily Post about what to do when you accuse a board chairman of homicide, criminal assault, and perjury. Or about what the board chairman should do, either.

It was Feuerman who finally found a way out of this awkward little social dilemma. "I'm going now. I hope you come to your senses, all of you." Before any of us could say or do another thing, he turned on his heel and strode off.

"Shouldn't we try to stop him?" asked Terry.

"How?" Jackie countered. "Call the police?"

"No, my dears," Sally Boyle said tiredly. "It's really up to me. I'll have a word with my nephew in the morning."

"Your nephew?"

"My sister's youngest. In the Justice Department. The criminal division. He's the assistant attorney general in charge."

"How will we know that you've done this, Mrs. Boyle?" Ralph asked.

"I don't understand," Sally said. But she did understand. "Very well. I suppose one of you had better come with me."

"It was the night Jackie got stabbed," I said in the Wild West Lounge at the motel. "I sat thinking about everything people had told us, and I suddenly realized that while the things they'd said about each other didn't add up, they'd all said basically the same thing about Feuerman."

"Which was?" Terry asked.

"Which was that on the eve of the deal that was going to make him rich and happy, he was down in the dumps. Depressed. Feeling sorry for himself.

"At first, I didn't remember much one way or the other about the state of his mind. But eventually it came back to me that at dinner that night Feuerman was quite cheerful, the way you'd expect him to feel. Then he left the table to go see Boyle."

"Didn't he say something about 'his master's voice'?" Jackie asked.

"I think he did. Anyway, when he came back he was a lot more subdued. And he really dug into that ice cream. Now, why the change of mood? The only reason I could think of was that Boyle had told him he was doing what he'd threatened to do the morning before, canceling the Swain's Bank deal."

"It could have been just a letdown," said Ralph.

"It could have been," I said. "But then there was the note."

"The note? But the note was about Shaver, not Feuerman."

"The note said, 'Shaver' on one line. Then on another line it says, 'give him a hundred.'"

"That's right," Ralph said.

"You can read it the way we all read it at the time. As if Boyle was reminding himself to give Shaver something. Or . . ."

"Come on," Terry demanded. "Out with it."

"Shaver was Boyle's lawyer. What if Boyle's note, instead of being *about* Shaver, was about something Boyle wanted Shaver to do?"

"Like, 'Tell Shaver to give somebody else a hundred?'" David said.

"Exactly."

"Who? And a hundred what?"

"Suppose Boyle *had* killed the deal. Might he not tell Shaver to pay Feuerman something for his time and trouble?"

"Sounds pretty farfetched to me," said Terry.

"That's why I went to see Shaver."

"And Shaver told you you were right?"

"Not exactly," I admitted. "Shaver's a lawyer, and lawyers never tell anybody anything if they can help it."

"You better believe it. So?"

"So I didn't ask Shaver about Feuerman directly. I asked him if anybody's status had changed significantly between the time the Swain's Bank negotiations started and Boyle's death."

"And he said yes?"

"He said, 'I can't substantiate that,' meaning yes. But he's a real cutie. He's in on the bank deal, too, and he doesn't want to rock the boat even a little bit. The way he put it was that the person whose status might have been in question was a major player at the start and is a major player now."

"But what you're saying is . . ."

"The way I read Shaver, Boyle didn't want to kill the deal. I was wrong about that. He wanted the deal to go ahead, but he wanted Feuerman out of it. Why, I don't know. It could be that Boyle just had to prove who was boss."

"It could be something else," said Jackie. "Boyle was all set to break off with Kitty. After that scene at lunch, maybe Boyle decided that he'd never be able to get rid of Kitty unless he got rid of Everett Feuerman too."

"I doubt that we'll ever find out," I said. "But, anyway, the 'hundred' in the note is probably a hundred thousand dollars. That's what Boyle was going to ask Shaver to pay Feuerman. That's what Boyle told Feuerman he was going to get instead of the millions of dollars he was expecting to get. Feuerman had to move fast to save himself. And he did."

I thought I deserved a certain amount of, well, praise for my superb powers of deduction. Wouldn't you? But all I got from Ralph was: "God. How do you think you're going to explain all *that* to a jury?"

You can't win.

I waved, and the waitress in the pony-skin vest and purple bandana brought us our check for five El Rancho Burgers, five Campfire Coffees and David's Gaucho Special, featured on the menu as "a Wrangler-Sized Slab of Mexican-Style Apple Pie Topped With a Scoop of our South of the Border Tequila-Vannila Ice Cream, $4.85." The spelling of *vanilla* is their responsibility, not mine. What the waitress thought of the five people in bedraggled formal wear who'd descended on the otherwise deserted Wild West Lounge at ten thirty in the evening to talk about a murder, I cannot imagine.

"Never mind what Ralph says," Jackie said tenderly, up in our room with the DO NOT DISTURB sign on the door. "I think you're brilliant. But poor Mrs. Boyle."

"You don't like her," I said.

There was a long interruption, during which we managed to kiss each other thoroughly, simultaneously remove substantial portions of superfluous clothing including but not limited to shoes and hosiery, and switch off the television set.

"I do like her," Jackie said. It took me several seconds to remember who she was talking about and considerably longer for my heartbeat to subside. "Or rather, I feel terribly sorry for her but no, I don't like her."

"Well, which is it?" I said.

"She has her own set of laws, doesn't she? I mean, our laws say that when you find out your son's mistress has just shot him dead, you have to tell the police. But Sally Boyle looks in *her* lawbook and smiles and decides, 'No, I don't want to do that, and under Law Thirteen about family scandal and disgrace, I don't have to.'"

"I suppose you've got a point," I said unhappily.

"All her life she's played by her rules, not ours. She doesn't parade it, but that's what she does. And she's so damn lovable that people let her get away with it. I'd be tempted myself. But it's wrong, because if she can do it, so can Feuerman. So can anybody."

"Sally Boyle's an outlaw, is that what you're saying?"

"Yes." Jackie stretched out a bare arm and snapped off the light. "Pardner, she rides the owl-hoot trail."

E P I L O G U E

$\mathcal{T}$hree mornings later, Ray Gerard showed up at the apartment. Jackie and I were eating breakfast, but he wouldn't join us. "I just came by to show you this," he said.

He handed me a single sheet of lined yellow paper from a legal pad, folded in thirds and then in half. On it were three lines in tiny handwriting.

"Boyle's?" I asked.

Gerard nodded.

I read aloud slowly. "'One: F out except as cons.'"

"He means consultant," Gerard said.

"'Two: One hundred K fee one-time. Three: Try to find F other work.'"

Corroboration. Solid, unambiguous corroboration.

"Where did this come from?"

"It was in his shirt pocket. It came back from Nye along with his other stuff."

"Turn it over to Mrs. Boyle's nephew at the Justice Department," I said promptly.

"Yeah," Gerard said. "It's kind of tough on Mrs. Boyle. But that's what I think too."

The story broke two days after that. The New York *Post* ran the biggest headline: FEDS TO PROBE SOCIALITE SLAYING. *The New York Times*, obviously torn between its lust for readership and its sense of perspective, felt that the lead stories of the day should probably be *(a)* the forthcoming summit conference, and *(b)* the indications that thirty-six million years from now the earth would be struck by a gigantic meteor and all life, except of course for the cockroach, would be extinguished. Accordingly, the *Times* put its story on the Miami grand jury investigation of Boyle's killing on page one, but in the lower left-hand corner below the fold.

Ramón the super had the *Post* in his hand when he waddled out to welcome us back from the supermarket. Politely, not wanting to interrupt, he watched Jackie exert all her strength to heave open the lobby door. He watched me work the cart packed with groceries over the doorjamb and down the three decorative marble steps. During this maneuver, one bottle did fall out of the cart, but it was plastic and didn't break. Ramón rolled it over to me with his foot. I picked it up and put it back in the cart.

"Mr. French, you see the paper?" He waved it languidly.

I said I had.

"This Boyle, he's the guy you were on the boat with him?"

"We both were," Jackie said, "and Terry and Ralph and David."

"Yeah, right. Gonna be heavy stuff, this grand jury, huh?"

"Probably," I said.

"They gonna come here, you think?"

"Who, the grand jury?" I asked. I didn't understand.

Jackie did, though. "It's okay, Ramón. Don't worry, no

cops. They're not going to come around here to talk to us. We'll probably all have to go back down there."

Ramón looked happier. "You mean Miami?"

"Miami."

"Hey, listen, Mr. French, Mrs. French. You're nice people."

"We're going to be real busy in Miami, Ramón," I said warningly.

"All you have to do, you just meet my cousin Resurrección at the airport. You know my cousin Innocénte?" Indeed we do. Innocénte is the relief doorman and also the account executive in charge of chrome trim and hood ornaments. No human being has ever worn a more blatantly inappropriate name. "So Resurrección, he's Innocénte's brother, he's good people, Mr. French."

"I'm sure he's a delightful individual," I said.

Ramón permitted a shocked expression to appear on his face. "Mr. French. What do you think we're talking about? We don't do no *farmacia*." Even I knew he meant drugs. "All you do, just bring back a little package, got pictures inside. You know, color prints."

"What of?" I said.

"Oh, you know, things."

"I can imagine," said Jackie.

"Oh, no, nothing bad. No kids, nothing like that."

"All the same, I think you'd better find another messenger," I said.

"Sure, no problem, I understand." As a special token of his esteem, he pressed the elevator button for us and kept his finger on it to hold the door open while we bumped our groceries inside. He took the dollar I gave him with a professional nod. Then he suddenly said, "I almost forgot. You know that piano belonged to Mrs. Rosensweig? I got nineteen hundred dollars for it and the guy come and took it away. Good, eh?"

"Terrific," I said. "Congratulations."

Ramón took his finger off the button and let the door

close. As slowly and uncertainly as always, its chains rattling, the elevator bore us aloft. I leaned over the grocery cart and gave Jackie a kiss on her ear. "Be it ever so humble," we caroled, together but slightly off key, "there's no place like home."